Love, Lucie x

Marita Conlon-McKenna

Love, Lucie x

SIMON AND SCHUSTER

First published in Great Britain in 2012 by Simon and Schuster UK Ltd
A CBS COMPANY

Text copyright © 2012 Marita Conlon-McKenna
Section break illustrations © Linzie Hunter 2012
Interior doodle illustrations © Laura Hope 2012
Designed by Paul Coomey

With special thanks to Clara Chambers
for designing Lucie's Mother's Day card

If you try any of the recipes in this book, always
ask a grown up to help you when using an oven

1 3 5 7 9 10 8 6 4 2

Simon & Schuster UK Ltd
1st Floor, 222 Gray's Inn Road
London
WC1X 8HB

Simon & Schuster Australia, Sydney

Simon & Schuster India, New Delhi

A CIP catalogue record for this book is available from the British Library.

TPB ISBN: 978-0-85707-833-9
PB ISBN: 978-0-85707-834-6
eBook ISBN: 978-0-85707-835-3

Printed and bound by CPI Group (UK) Ltd, Croydon, CR0 4YY

www.simonandschuster.co.uk
www.simonandschuster.com.au

For Mandy, Laura, Fiona and James

Autumn

Dear Mum,

Today is the day of your funeral; the saddest day in the whole world. It began to rain before breakfast and it kept raining all morning. I think even the sky was sad!

A big black funeral car came to collect us and we all had to make a run with our umbrellas from the house to the car, from the car to the church and then later to the graveyard. The rain was pounding down . . . pelting us, soaking us; the water running everywhere, down our coats, shoes, jackets, hair . . . running down our faces so it was hard to tell the rain from our tears.

When we were getting dressed this morning Dad said that things were bad enough without him having to see the three of us dressed in black. He said that you would want us to wear our prettiest dresses.

Mum, I wore my pale pink dress with the rosebuds and my green wrap and ballerina shoes. Chloe wore her cute purple dress with the puffed sleeves Hugo had his new shirt and jacket and Dad his cream jacket and your favourite red and gold tie. We looked like we were going to a party not a funeral.

When we got to the church it was crowded with all our relations and friends. Our neighbours, schoolfriends, Dr Nicholls and even some of the nurses who helped to look after you, everyone turned up. Me and Dad and Chloe and Hugo had to sit up in the front row of the church with Mémé and Poppa beside us and Uncle Theo and Auntie Clara in the row right behind. I didn't like sitting at the front, but at least it meant that people could only see our backs and not our faces. Mémé bought a big packet of tissues in her handbag as she knew we'd need them.

There were flowers everywhere: pink and red roses and bunches of those big pink frothy flowers you like from the garden. The church choir sang your favourite songs and Dad put the photo of you that he took last summer when we all went sailing on top of the coffin – the one where you're laughing, the wind blowing your hair.

In the church Uncle Theo spoke and Chloe, Hugo and I said a prayer up on the altar too. Then, at the end, Dad stood up and talked about you and everyone cried and clapped. After the funeral we walked down the church behind the big wooden box that held you and for a moment I thought that maybe I wouldn't be able to breathe, but then Hugo squeezed my hand so hard that it hurt and Dad held on to my other hand. I could feel his pulse beating strong and hard, his skin warm and firm, not cold and smooth like yours when I touched it. . .

Then everyone went to the graveyard and I closed my eyes in the big black car as we drove through the village. We passed your favourite café, my school, and the bookshop where you worked with Tess and Mr Humphrey. The shop was closed, the blinds drawn.

The graveyard was big and surrounded by tall trees, their leaves turning gold and red and orange. The rain stopped and the sun came out the minute we got out of the car and walked to a place where the earth was all dug up, and then they lowered your coffin into the ground. Down . . . down . . . down. . .

Father Lennon said more prayers and Chloe and Dad and Hugo and I stood there watching and then threw the roses we picked from the garden into your grave. Down . . . down . . . down . . . falling on top of you.

Back at the house it was crowded. All the cousins and aunts and uncles and the neighbours, even old Mr and Mrs O'Grady, came. Roz and Auntie Trish and Auntie Maria helped organise the food – there was chicken cooked in a sauce and rice and salad. Chloe and I helped to pass round the plates.

Granny had two whiskies and cried and Poppa had a cognac, a Napoleon Brandy; he said if it was good enough for Bonaparte to survive the Russian winters it might be strong enough to help him get through the day. Everyone kept shaking my hand and saying sorry. Sorry- sorry- sorry, but why are they sorry? They didn't do anything! They didn't make you sick! It wasn't their fault that the hospital and doctors and nurses couldn't make you better! That you were so sick you had to leave us and go to heaven.

My teacher Mrs Martin came to the church too, and my whole class. They sat near the back. Hugo's friends Jonathan and Mark and Conor stayed close to him all day like three strong bodyguards protecting him, and Chloe had her friends and her new boyfriend Tim. I don't think she wanted you or Dad to know about him yet, but now that you are in heaven

you probably know everything, about him and Chloe and everyone!

Now it's late; everyone has gone except for the family. They're all downstairs: Granny and Granddad, Poppa and Mémé, Uncle Alan and Auntie Trish, Auntie Maria, Julie, Uncle Theo and Auntie Clara talking about you and drinking red wine and eating the smelly cheese that you love with crackers and bread. Mémé carried it in her handbag on the plane all the way from Paris. The other people must have thought; *Who is that silly old French woman that smells!* You know I hate that cheese. I will never eat it.

'I can't believe Madeleine is gone!' That's what everyone keeps saying, over and over again. No one can believe it. That you are dead, that you have left us. I don't believe it either. Mum, I keep thinking you are in the next room, busy in the kitchen or working at your computer in the office, and in a few minutes you will come in and stroke my arm or fiddle with my hair and say: 'Lucie, have you seen my reading glasses?' or 'Lucie, be a pet and run and get my cardigan, please!'

I can still hear them laughing and telling stories about you. About when you were a little girl in France, and how you met and fell in love with Dad.

Dad told the story about when you brought Chloe home from the hospital and she cried and cried, and you didn't know what to do with such a baby, and you put on rock music and danced with her up and down the living room floor for hours until she stopped crying and smiled at you. Everyone laughed at that because it was so like you to think of something like that. Then he told the story about how I bit your nose when I was a baby getting my first teeth because I wanted to chew on something and loved your long bony nose. And then Chloe remembered the time you went shopping and forgot little Hugo and left him in the supermarket looking at the toys, and you only remembered him when you were lifting the shopping bags out of the car at home and you said to Chloe: 'Where's your brother?' You drove so fast back to the shops that a policeman almost stopped the car, but when you got there Hugo was happy in the shop playing with the Lego! He didn't even know that you had gone. So many stories, but I couldn't listen any more, so I came up here.

It's nearly midnight and they are still talking downstairs. Hugo has come upstairs now and is asleep on the camp bed in my bedroom and Chloe is going to sleep on the couch bed in the study. Uncle Theo and Auntie Clara have Chloe's room and Max and Mathieu are in the bunk beds in Hugo's and Mémé and Poppa are in the spare bedroom.

My eyes are sore from crying and my throat hurts. I'm in my pyjamas and ready for bed. Dad is downstairs and you are not here to tuck me in, so I tuck myself in and pretend I can smell your perfume and hear your voice and that you are near and beside me, and not far away at all.

Good night, Mum.

Love,
Lucie x

P.S. I HATE FUNERALS!

Mum,

This morning I could feel you.

You were so close beside me, like you were sitting on the edge of my bed, watching me. I wanted to wake up and talk to you, but was frightened that would make you go away so I stayed half awake, watching and feeling you. You looked down at Hugo on the camp bed. He was still sleeping and his quilt was on the floor where he had kicked it during the night. I thought about how he looked so small to have no mother . . . and I knew you were watching him too.

I wanted to call Chloe or Dad to tell them that you were here with us, but I didn't want to break the magic . . . to make you disappear or go away. . . Then I must have gone back to sleep. When I woke up it was nearly lunchtime. I looked to see if you left me a sign or something, but I couldn't find a trace of you. Mum, why didn't you leave a sign? Next time you come you must leave a sign.

Everyone was so tired today and slept in. Uncle Theo was the only one up early and he took Mathieu and Max out to look around the city. They wanted to see the Viking boats and weapons and the ancient bog bodies in the museum.

Poor Mémé had a bad headache and stayed in bed. Chloe said it was no wonder as she was crying all night.

We had brunch and Poppa and Dad cooked sausages and rashers and fried potato and eggs, while Auntie Clara and Chloe and I tried to tidy up a bit. The house is really messy after so many people coming yesterday. It looked like we had a big party with all the glasses and plates and wine bottles. Not a funeral!

I don't want to annoy you, but someone spilled a big glass of red wine on the carpet in the living room . . . but you probably know that already.

Later, Dad and Mémé and Poppa wanted to go back to the graveyard to see your grave so we all went. Today it was quiet; it felt so different to yesterday. Your grave is in a really sunny spot and the men who worked there had taken away the green wooden board and had shovelled the earth on top of your coffin. Covering you with the heavy earth . . . it must feel awful. Does it?

The top of your grave was covered with bunches of flowers: so many of them from so many friends with messages and little cards. We gathered them up.

'It is like a pretty florist's shop,' Mémé said.

It is so peaceful and nice there, but very lonely.

Dad said that in a few weeks we will get a headstone for your grave so everyone will know who you are and how much we all love and miss you.

When we got home poor Mémé went back to bed and Poppa Henri dozed on the couch. When Max and Mathieu came home they just wanted to play more computer games. Hugo wanted to play too but Max pushed him out of the room. They ended up having a big wrestling match on the floor! I bet Hugo's glad that he's got sisters.

Tonight it felt like everything was in slow motion. Auntie Clara heated up more of the chicken and rice for dinner. The fridge and freezer are full of stuff to eat as all the neighbours keep bringing us lasagnes and pies and tarts. They think that food helps. Dad says he is very grateful and it means that we won't have to worry about cooking for a while.

After dinner everyone stayed up late again, sitting round the table and talking, going over everything that has happened. Mémé said that you should have listened to her and gone to a proper hospital in Paris, or taken her friend Sybil's advice and gone to America. Mémé said that the best hospitals in the world are there. Dad said that you had the best specialists trying to help and that the doctors and nurses and everyone did everything they could to make you better, but it didn't work . . . it just didn't work.

Then everyone started to talk about what they loved most about you. Auntie Clara said that you were very brave, the bravest woman she ever met.

Uncle Theo said that you were the best big sister and that even when you and he were kids you always stuck together. He said he used to follow you around, but you didn't mind because you were always the kindest one in the family . . . the one who looked after everyone.

Mathieu said you were a great aunt because you never forgot birthdays or Christmas presents and always knew what they were doing.

Max said you always told him funny jokes, and sent him brilliant books to read.

Poppa said that you were the best daughter a man could have.

Mémé said that you were not only the best daughter,

but also the most wonderful mother and that you were so proud of Chloe and Hugo and me.

Dad says you were far more than his wife ... you were his best friend.

Chloe said you were our mum and we would never forget you.

Hugo said he loved the way you smelled and the way you tickled him and showed him how to ride his bike.

I didn't know what to say first; there are too many things that I love about you. I love your voice and the sound of your feet. I love the way you sing and play the guitar and I love you for just being you and because you are my mum.

Everyone cried and then Poppa started to blow his nose and Uncle Theo blew his harder until we ended up having a big nose-blowing competition. It was a tie between Max and Poppa over who won.

Then we made popcorn and sang some songs. Dad said no sad songs tonight, only funny or happy ones, and that everyone had to sing, even if they couldn't sing at all (like Uncle Theo).

It was a sad night . . . a funny night . . . all about everyone missing you.

Poppa drank more brandy and Mémé said that if I wanted I could have a little wine with some water in it *a la française*. I tasted it and it was awful. I will never, ever drink wine as I prefer Coca-Cola.

Now I'm writing to you in my bedroom and Hugo is snoring again on the small camp bed. I can't sleep with the noise. I hold his nose, but he only stops breathing for a second and then turns back and snores again. . .

Love,
Lucie x

Saturday 24th September

Dear Mum,

I feel so sad and miss you so much.

Lots of people keep calling to the house and phoning,
and there are always people around trying to talk and
bringing flowers and food. Dad says they are trying to be
nice, but I wish that they would just go away and leave us
alone.

I feel so lonely all the time without you.

I'm so sad . . . but taking out my paper and pen and
writing to you like this makes me feel you are near and I
can talk to you, and tell you things like I always did.

Love,

Lucie x

Dear Mum,

At church this morning Father Lennon said a special prayer for you. Chloe squeezed my hand really hard so we would be strong and not cry as some of the kids from my school were there.

Afterwards we all went to Granny and Granddad's for Sunday lunch. Granny made a big fuss over Mémé and made her sit in her big blue armchair in the sitting room. The room is full of family photos of Dad and us with you which made Mémé upset. 'Why did God take my beautiful daughter and not an old lady like me?'

'Maybe he didn't want a difficult old woman like you?' Poppa Henri teased gently, giving her a big hug and kiss.

Uncle Alan and Auntie Trish and Auntie Maria and Julie all came for lunch today so Granddad put the dining table and kitchen table together so that everyone could fit, and Granny used her best pretty flower plates and the good linen tablecloth.

'Everyone is very welcome to our home today,' Granddad

said before we ate; his voice sounded funny and I could tell he was trying not to cry. 'It only seems like yesterday that our David met a beautiful young French girl who had come to Ireland to learn English. Mary and I were happy to welcome Madeleine into our home and into our hearts, and when Madeleine and David married we were delighted to be united with the Aubert family. There have been so many family celebrations since then; christenings, birthdays, communions, summer parties. It's so sad that we come together today in our home because of Madeleine's death, but I think she would want the connection between the two families to always remain. Mary and I want everyone to know that Celine and Henri, Theo and Clara and the boys will always be welcome under this roof.' Everyone clapped and there was food and wine and lemonade and jugs of orange with ice.

After lunch, we went out in the garden. We found Granddad's old croquet set and played a game, with the boys against the girls. We won.

When we got home Uncle Theo, Auntie Clara and the boys had to pack as they are leaving for the airport early in the morning. Uncle Theo said we all had to promise to come and see them in France during the summer.

The last few days the house has been crowded with people . . . busy, noisy, so it will be very strange when it is just back to us. I don't want to think about it.

Mum, I wish that you were still here with us.
Love,
Lucie x

Dear Mum,

Uncle Theo and Auntie Clara and the boys are gone. Hugo misses them, but at least he is back in his bedroom again. People still keep calling to the house.

Yesterday a lady called Leah came round. She said that you were in a book club together and that you both always loved the same books and films. She got upset so Dad made her coffee.

Amy came over today after school on her bicycle. She brought me a box of chocolate Rice Krispie cakes she'd made. Her eyes were red and she looked like she had been crying.

'I'm going to miss your mum so much,' she said and began to cry all over again. I had to get her a tissue from the box in Chloe's room. Every time Amy looked at anything in the house she looked like she was going to cry again.

I feel like crying too, but my eyes are too sore. I need my best friend to be fun . . . to be happy . . . not to be sad!! Mum, do you think I'm being mean to Amy or should I just let her cry all over the house when she sees your photo or the chair you love or the cushion cover you made? She's my best friend and I don't want her to make me feel even worse.

I wanted to go out so we went for a big cycle through the park and up by the little woods. We sat for a while under the trees. There were chestnuts everywhere and we gathered loads of conkers. I found a massive one for Hugo.

Amy asked if I wanted to talk about you, but I said, 'No thank you. Not today.' I wanted to cycle and feel the air in my face and the pedals at my feet and see all the trees and greenery whizzing by. Talking about what's happened is not going to change things. It is not going to bring you back. I just want things to be ordinary again . . . that is if we can ever go back to that . . . I don't know. Amy told me about when her granny died three years ago and how sad she felt then.

'Did it get better?' I asked. She said it did. She still thinks about her granny and misses her a lot, but is not sad about it any more. But maybe it is different when it is your granny?

Amy said everyone in school was asking about me. Mrs Martin told Amy she is to show me the homework she has done when I go back to school next week so I will be able to catch up. At least I missed the big maths test they

had yesterday. Amy said it was horrible and that Becky
O'Connor started crying because she couldn't answer any
of the questions.

When it started to get dark we cycled back to my house.
Dad asked Amy if she wanted to stay for tea but she had
to go home.

Tonight Mémé made risotto with mushrooms and peas. It
tasted good, but not as nice as yours.

Mémé doesn't want to leave us and go back to France
tomorrow, but Poppa says that they must. They have
things to attend to in Paris. Besides, they will be back
again and we will all go and stay with them during *les
vacances*.

Everything is changing. I wish that it didn't. I hope Dad
still wants to go to France every year like we always do,
otherwise we'll end up hardly ever seeing Mémé and Poppa.

Please don't let that happen, Mum.

Love,
Lucie x

Dear Mum,

Mémé and Poppa went back to Paris today. It was awful as Mémé was so upset. She didn't want to go home and wanted to stay here with us.

'How can I leave with my little Madeleine lying in the ground?' she said when Poppa tried to put the cases in Dad's car. 'My child is here . . . this is where I should stay.'

Everyone felt bad and Chloe told Mémé that we love having her here staying with us, but that Max and Mathieu might need her too. We promised that we will all go to France during the summer like we always do. Poor Mémé and Poppa, they both look so old and tired as if all the colour and life has gone out of them.

Eventually Mémé put on her coat and took her handbag. Chloe and I went to the airport with them and Hugo went to play next door with Conor.

The airport was busy and we helped Mémé with her luggage. She has suddenly become an old lady who needs us to help her.

It was strange coming home and knowing that nobody was in our house except for us. It seemed so quiet and still. The house has been so full of people for so long – nurses and doctors and visitors. Everyone coming to see you and talk to you and help you and now suddenly everyone is gone and it is back to just being us, but instead of there being five of us . . . now there are only four.

Dad made toasted cheese sandwiches for dinner and then went back to do some more work. When I went to find him he was asleep in the chair in his study, but Chloe said to leave him because he was exhausted. We all are and we went to bed early.

I like writing to you, telling you things. Sometimes I think I am better at writing things than saying things. It's easier to write things on the page than to speak them. You said that's what some of the great writers and poets do when they put their words on the page.

Mum, I wish you didn't die, I wish you were here with us all. It's so lonely without you.

Love,
Lucie x

30th September

Mum,

Come back! Come back, please come back to us. . .
Even if it is only for a day or a few hours.

Just don't leave us forever.

Love,
Lucie x

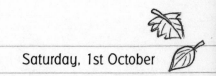

Saturday, 1st October

Mum,

I saw you today out in the garden. You were standing quiet and still, looking at the house.

The leaves are falling from the trees and you walked across the pile of leaves on the grass. I could hear the noise of them as you passed. I waved to you and called you, but you didn't say anything, you just kept looking at the house before disappearing. I pulled on my slippers and ran as fast as I could in my pyjamas outside to the garden, but you were gone.

Dad came out a few minutes later and asked me what I was doing outside. I told him that I saw you.

'Mum's not here, Lucie. She's gone from us. We have to let her go.'

'But I saw her.'

'Come back inside. It's far too early to be up on a chilly morning like this. You'll catch a cold.'

Dad made me go back in.

I watched for you all the rest of the day.

Love,

Lucie x

Dear Mum,

Today we went back to school. It was awful as we all wanted to stay home but Dad says we have to try to get back to normal again. I don't think that anything will ever be normal again!

Dad promised that if we needed him, or if there were any problems, Mrs Keeling would phone him and he would come and get us immediately. It felt strange walking into school . . . like everyone was looking at us and secretly talking about us.

Poor Lucie. . .

Poor Hugo. . .

Didn't you hear that their mother died?

I hung my coat on my peg in the corridor and walked down to Hugo's classroom with him. He looked so pale and scared that I could nearly count the freckles on his face. He didn't want me to leave him at first, but Mr Loftus his teacher and Jonathan both came along and after a few minutes he was fine.

By the time I got to my classroom everyone was sitting at

their desks. I walked in with my head down and tried not to look at anyone until I sat at my desk beside Amy. I could feel everyone's eyes staring at me. Mrs Martin looked really sad, like she was the one going to cry, not me.

'Everyone, I'd like to welcome Lucie back today.' She said, 'We all know how sad things have been for Lucie and her family recently so I want everyone in this class to be especially nice and kind to Lucie. We are all her friends.'

I just stared at my desk.

Amy grabbed my hand and squeezed it, and when I looked at her she had tears in her eyes. My eyes are so sore and tired and dry that I don't have any more tears left to cry.

I didn't want to be rude though so I said thank you to Mrs Martin. Sitting there with everyone looking at me made me wish that I had never gone to school and had just stayed in my pyjamas in bed at home instead.

I tried to do some work, but for the rest of the morning I could hardly think and I didn't want to talk to anyone except Amy.

At breaktime I went to the bathroom and stayed there and didn't go back till I heard the bell ring.

Then at lunchtime I tried to eat my salami and lettuce sandwich. All the girls from my class came up to talk to me, but I just kept eating. After lunch we went out in the yard to play. The girls wanted me to sit on one of the benches and talk to them. Tell them about what happened. But I don't want to talk.

I asked Ben and Sean if Amy and I could play football with them and the rest of the boys. Usually Ben would say no, but maybe he remembered what Mrs Martin said because they let us play! I ran up and down the yard, racing to get the ball. I ran so fast that it hurt and I could hardly breathe.

Dad left work early and collected us from school.

'Are you going to come home early every day, Dad?' Hugo asked.

'Just for the next few days.'

Dad said that we are going to get a minder to come to the house after school to look after us. Otherwise Hugo and I will have to go next door to Roz's or Granny will have to come over some days. I wish that you were here then we wouldn't need a minder. Instead you'd be waiting for us after school like always, or coming to collect us in the car if it was raining. I don't want to get a minder.

Everyone was cool to Chloe in her school today. Even Lisa

Flynn, one of the meanest girls in her class, was nice to her and she got no homework, which isn't fair as Hugo and I both got homework!

Chloe and Dad made tacos again. I like them, but not almost every night. If we get a minder maybe they can cook and do other things in the house.

I wish that you were here.

Today was a very hard day . . . I'm glad it's over. Dad says that tomorrow will be a bit easier. I hope so!

Love,
Lucie x

Friday 7th October

Dear Mum,

I'm so glad that the week is over! Why do I have to go to school, Mum? I hate it!

I hate it because I know that you'll never, ever bring me to school or collect me from school again. Never say: 'Lucie, do your homework,' or 'How was class? What did you learn today?' or 'What do you want in your lunch box?'

Everything has changed and everyone keeps asking over and over again if I am OK and I say yes to them, but I'm not.

It's not getting easier. It's too hard. I spent all of today and yesterday just wanting to find Hugo and go home.

The only time that things don't feel so bad is when I play football in the yard because then I don't have to think. But I can't play football all the time. I don't think I'm ever going to feel better. . .

Love,
Lucie x

Mum,

I hate Chloe. She is the meanest big sister anyone could have!

It's not fair that just because you are not here she keeps picking on me and bossing me. She thinks I am her slave! Well, I'm not. She says I have to do this and do that! Do what she tells me! Load the dishwasher, empty the dishwasher, sweep the kitchen floor, hoover, tidy up . . . I told her I have lots of homework, but she says that doesn't matter.

Just because she is older than me she keeps telling me what to do. She thinks that she is in charge, but she's not!

Dad won't listen and says we have to sort it out between us and stop fighting. But how can you stop fighting with someone like Chloe? Some days she drives me crazy.

Aaarrghh . . . this is one of them.

Love,
Lucie x

Mum,

I watched a programme on the TV about kids that are home-schooled and just stay home and read and learn and study and get lessons on their computer. It sounded kind of cool and I wish that Dad could do that with us, then we wouldn't have to go to school every day and could just stay home forever.

Dad laughed when I asked him about it and said: 'Who is going to work and pay the bills then?'

I spoke to Hugo about it and he said he wants to go to school and see his friends and play football and not stay home in this sad house all the time.

I like being home because here I don't have to pretend I'm fine all the time.

When I put on my school uniform I have to pretend that I am OK and go to class and do work and hang out with my friends, but I'm not OK!

I don't want to be there with them. I just want to be home

where I am near you and don't have to pretend. . .

 I don't want to go to school tomorrow.

Love,

Lucie x

Tuesday 11th October

Mum,

  I saw you again.

  You were sitting on the couch reading a book. I wanted to run over and hug you and touch you and talk to you, but you acted as if you didn't see me and just kept reading. I was frightened to breathe and I just watched as you turned the pages. Then you looked up·and smiled at me, but when I went towards you . . . you just disappeared.

  I waited for ages and ages for you to come back, but you didn't and then Chloe came in and turned on some stupid programme on the TV. I told her to get out of the room but she wouldn't.

Please come back again. It doesn't matter if we can talk or not, I just want to see you.

Love,
Lucie x

Mum,

It's awful but sometimes at school I feel so upset that I have to go to the bathroom. Mrs Martin lets Amy come with me. I get a pain in my throat from trying not to cry. Chloe says she feels the same . . . it is awful. People talk about their mums all the time which makes it harder.

It's stupid (and I know you will think that I am mean) but I get jealous that they still have a mum.

It was really wet today so Dad collected us from school. Next week he has to work full days again so Granny and Roz are going to mind us after school instead.

On Monday Granny will collect Hugo as I have Book Club and I'll walk home with Chloe. Hugo and I will go next door to Roz's on Tuesday and Thursday after school as Chloe has basketball. We'll walk home with Conor and Killian, but if it's wet Roz will collect us. Granny will collect me from school on Wednesday as Hugo has football practice, and then we will collect him later. Granny will stay and make dinner for us all at our house and on Friday we will all go to Granny and Granddad's house. It's a lot to remember! Dad bought a big new Weekly Planner thing for the kitchen and has everyone's schedule written down.

'How am I supposed to remember what everyone is doing and where you are every day?' He said, 'It's bad enough trying to manage my own work schedule and meetings, but then trying to tie in with everyone else is a nightmare!'

'Mum did it,' Hugo said.

Dad looked a bit sad then. 'I know . . . but I'm not as organised as her.'

We put everything we could remember on the planner: birthdays, parties, school holidays, Chloe's basketball matches, Hugo's football practices, swimming lessons, even dentist visits and our parent-teacher meetings. Dad's new planner looks very full already.

'We just have to follow this and make sure everything is covered and no one gets forgotten about,' he said.

None of us want to be forgotten about.

'Then every week I'll shop online and get the groceries delivered and anything else we need we can pick up in the local shops.'

Dad said that we all have to help and pull together. We are still a family. I wish you were here and everything didn't have to change so much.

Mum, I wish things were still the same.

Bonne nuit,
Lucie x

Dear Mum,

Hugo sleeps with a light on in his room now and we always check there is nothing scary hanging anywhere because he keeps having bad dreams. Last week he thought his fleece jacket was a man standing near the door waiting to catch him.

Tonight he had a bad dream again. Dad had to go out so Chloe and her boyfriend Tim were babysitting. They were downstairs watching a film so I let Hugo get into bed with me. I told him it was OK and that he could stay the night with me. Sometimes he can't remember his bad dreams or what made him scared, but he gets really upset and cries out.

Sometimes he dreams weird things, about monsters or people turning into zombies or vampires when they are dead. We keep telling him that it is all made up, but Hugo still dreams about them.

I love Hugo. I remember when you told us that we were getting a new baby. I said I wanted a girl, but I'm glad that I've got Hugo. One sister like Chloe is enough for anyone.

Hugo's funny and much nicer than most of my friends' brothers, but he's still so small and I hate it when he gets scared and upset.

Do you remember when I was little I used to get really scared too, of the big bad wolf? I used to wait for him to get me when I was asleep in bed, but Hugo's dreams are far worse. Dad says he has a big imagination which doesn't help things. To help him fall asleep I read him a few pages of my books. I try to find a boring bit or sing him a song until I see his eyes close. It usually works, but then I have to try to get to sleep as he kicks and turns in my bed and sticks his elbow in my back!

Big yawns. . .

Love,
Lucie x

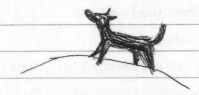

Mum,

Hugo and I went to Roz's after school.

She made us do our homework with the boys then they went out in the road to play, and I just stayed inside and watched stupid stuff on TV. Roz is really nice. She misses you so much and all the fun and laughs you had together.

'Good friends are very hard to come by, Lucie, always remember that.'

She asked how we are all doing and how are we coping without you.

I told her that we are OK . . . well, sort of.

I told her about Hugo's bad dreams about you being dead and in a coffin. I told her that sometimes Chloe doesn't sleep either and listens to music on her iPod nearly all night and that Dad stays up really late searching the internet on his laptop.

'What about you, Lucie?' she asked me. I told her how much I miss you, but how sometimes I know that you are still around me . . . I can feel it.

Roz wanted to know if me, Chloe or Hugo had talked to anybody about you. I didn't really know what she meant, but

I told her we talk to Granny and Auntie Trish a lot, and that I sometimes talked to Amy, but not to anyone else really.

'It's just that when we lose someone we love it's good to talk to someone outside of our family and friends, someone who is used to talking with people or kids who have lost someone,' Roz said.

I did think about what she said, but I don't want to talk to a stranger about the way I feel and how bad things are!

Then Roz showed me some of the photos she took at her photography class. They are really good. Roz says that she feels a camera can show and say much more than we think. There were some great photos of Conor and Killian and some of the woods which are all different colours, and one or two are in black and white.

Dad was dead late home so we had dinner at Roz's. She gave us some chicken curry to take home for Dad and Chloe. Mum, I really like Roz and we're so lucky that she is our next-door neighbour.

Love,
Lucie x

Wednesday 19th October

Dear Mum,

Granny collected me after school today and we went
to Starbucks and had a drink and a muffin and got some
groceries before going back to collect Hugo from football
practice.

He was so muddy that Granny made him take off his dirty
football boots and socks and shirt and throw them in the boot
of her car. I told her that you usually brought a change of
clothes for Hugo. She made Hugo have a hot shower when we
got home.

Granny vacuumed the hall and the living room and the
family room and got me to bring down a big wash basket
from upstairs and put on a wash. Then she made a big
shepherd's pie and I helped her to mash the potato and put
it on the top.

Chloe was in one of her bad moods when she came home
and went upstairs and turned on her music without even
saying hello. I told Granny that she's always like that lately.

Dad looked tired when he came home and Granny made him have a shower and change and then sit down to have dinner. 'Someone has to keep an eye on all of you,' she said.

When we sat down to eat Granny got annoyed because Chloe said she wasn't hungry and wouldn't eat any of her dinner. She wouldn't even taste it and just had a pot of yogurt.

Afterwards Granny stayed for ages talking to Dad while Hugo and I watched TV and Chloe went on the computer. She spends hours on Facebook with Tim and her friends!

I'm glad Granny was here today. It's nice having her here when we get back from school and having someone to make dinner instead of just getting takeaways or ready meals. I wish she could come every day.

Missing you so much.

Love,
Lucie x

Mum,

Today is your one month anniversary. Dad said he didn't want a big fuss, but Chloe and me went with him to your grave after school and said some prayers. We put fresh flowers on it and cleared away some of the fallen leaves.

Hugo didn't come with us and went to Granny's house instead. He keeps having bad dreams and I think Dad's worried about him.

Mum, I can't believe that it is a whole month since I talked to you and touched you and held your hand. Thirty days . . . it's so long since we all said goodbye to you and kissed you and you stopped breathing.

I pretend sometimes that you are back in hospital or only gone to visit Mémé and Poppa in France and will be home soon. Chloe said that she pretends you won a fabulous holiday and have gone off exploring around the world, but will be back any day.

Dad said that he wishes he could pretend, but unfortunately he can't. . . Poor Dad. . . Tonight I heard him crying in his room. He sounded so sad and upset that I wanted to go and see if he was OK, but Chloe said no. She said that Dad needs to cry. He's so lonely without you and he tries to pretend for us that everything is OK, but we know it isn't.

He's been so good helping all of us the last few weeks and no one has been there to help him. Mum, pleeeasse do something to make Dad feel better.

From your very sad daughter.

Love,
Lucie x

Dear Mum,

Mrs Martin asked to talk to me after class today. I thought that I was in *big trouble*, but she just wanted to find out how I was doing in school.

'Lucie, I know how hard it is for you to come back here to sit at your desk and try to do schoolwork,' she said, but I didn't know what to say to her.

'I understand a little how you must be feeling because I lost my husband five years ago. It was a terrible time and the only thing that kept me going was the small things, the day-to-day stuff. Teaching my class, marking homework, talking to my friends, just having to get up every day, put on my clothes and leave my house. All I really wanted was to stay home all the time and not go out, but doing those little things day by day helped. And sometimes it helps to just talk about it, so remember I'm here if you need someone to talk to.'

I really like Mrs Martin. She showed me a photo of her husband and she looked really sad. I think she is very lonely still.

I told her some days I can't concentrate or think or even remember stuff. She said that is OK, that I just need to take my time and do what I can. She said I'm clever and will catch up.

Can you believe that Mrs Martin thinks I'm clever! She's the nicest teacher ever.

Miss you so much!

Love,

Lucie x

Dear Mum,

Dad and Chloe had a MASSIVE FIGHT tonight. They were shouting so loudly I'm sure that Roz and the boys next door could hear them. Chloe says she hates him and our family and the way it is now, and Dad said: 'Well, that's all you've got, Chloe! And I'm here trying to do my best whether you like it or not.'

Chloe was really upset and slammed her bedroom door so hard that she almost broke it. She was crying for ages and ages and every time I knocked she told me to get lost, but I wouldn't . . . so I went in after a while.

She tried to push me out of the room, but I stood firm.

'I hate Dad! I hate this family!' she said. 'I really do.'

'Why?'

'Because it's all different now. We're not a proper family any more, you know that. You must feel it too. Dad thinks that by having lots of rules and timetables we can just be the same; carry on as normal. But nothing can ever be normal again. I'm fifteen and Dad thinks I'm just a kid like you and Hugo, that I have to do just what he says. He wants me to stay home all the time and babysit you two and do jobs around the house. Things would never be like this if Mum was here!'

I felt kind of guilty, as it's true that Dad is always asking Chloe to look after us if he has to go out or stay late at work. And he tells her to do lots of the washing and stuff too. No wonder she hates us all.

'I have a life!' she said to me. 'I have school and study and my friends and Tim. I'm not a kid any more whether Dad likes it or not. Mum understood, but he doesn't. I just wish Mum was still here with us.'

'You've still got me, Chloe,' I said really quietly and then I thought she was going to laugh or say something mean or try to push me out of the room again. But she just looked at me and said: 'Sometimes I miss her so much. It's so hard, Lucie. Too hard. . . '

I know what she meant. Not having you around is the worst, worst thing in the world. Some of my friends give out about their mums and moan all the time about them, but they don't know what it is like . . . *really* like . . . not to have one. . . Only we know that.

By the time we had finished talking Chloe had calmed

down. You always said talking not shouting is the best way.

'I'm sorry,' she said. 'I'm meant to be the big sister helping you and Hugo and I'm not doing a very good job of it, am I?' I told her that it was OK, that we would all look after each other.

We do have each other. You told us to stick together like the three musketeers no matter how bad things got and to stand up and fight for each other, not with each other. I guess that's what we have to try and do. Chloe patted the bed and I got in beside her like we used to when we were small.

'Do you think we'll ever see her again?' she asked me.

'Sure we will.'

'I don't know about that. I don't know if I believe any of that stuff . . . but I'd like to see her. . . '

I didn't know whether to tell Chloe that I see you sometimes and feel you near me as I didn't want to get her all upset again. I know Chloe's annoying, but can't you find a way to make her and Dad stop fighting about things and for her to feel that you are still close by her the way I do?

Love (and hugs),

Lucie x

Saturday 23rd October

Dear Mum,

Tonight Dad decided to make us all a 'proper dinner'. He got meat and carrots and onions and everything and spent ages cutting it all up and cooking it. Chloe and I asked if he wanted any help, but he said he was OK and that he was following your recipe.

The clothes baskets were all full, so Chloe and I tried to sort them out into what needed cleaning or washing or ironing urgently. I don't know what happened, the next thing we knew there was an awful smell coming from the kitchen, I think Dad must have been checking his emails on his iPhone, but he didn't notice that the beef stew was burning. All the meat got stuck to the big pot and the onion and carrot went all brown and yukky! We tried to make it better and add water but it was disgusting. It was stuck to the pot like glue and Chloe could hardly get any out. When we looked we saw the bottom of the pot (your favourite red one) was really burnt!

Dad kept shouting: 'I can't do it! I can't do this!' And then he flung the pot in the bin. 'I can't even cook a decent meal! I can't do things the way she did . . . How in God's name am I meant to do this?' He was so upset. 'I can't do this on my own!' he kept saying and went and sat over on the kitchen couch.

'Dad, you're not on your own,' I said. 'You have us!'

We told Dad we didn't care about the stupid stew!

Or if the house is messy!

Or if we have no clean clothes!

'We love you,' Chloe said. 'that's all that matters. We can all help. Do things. Tidy up, clean up, do the washing.'

Mum, when you were sick it seemed there were always people around the house helping and organising things, but now it's just the four of us on our own.

It's OK being on our own again, but we just need to get used to it.

Chloe made Dad a big mug of coffee. There wasn't much food left in the house so Chloe said she'd make cheese omelette for dinner instead. You showed her how to make it and it's the one thing she is really good at cooking. Chloe said she'd teach me how to cook them too.

Dad is doing his best. He really is. But he misses you so much.

We all do.

Today was a Very Bad Day.

Love,

Lucie x

Dear Mum,

There was a huge storm during the night. It blew down the maple tree in our back garden and two big branches from the big sycamore tree in Roz's garden and smashed the O'Grady's greenhouse. Your big blue flowerpot near the back door fell over too and got all cracked, but Dad said he'll get a new one in the garden centre and move all your plants and bulbs into it. The wind and the rain were so loud that we could hardly sleep so we all ended up in your room with Dad.

On the news it showed some huge trees that had fallen down and blocked roads, and some boats that got smashed on the rocks, and lots of buildings and houses that had the tiles blown off their roofs.

Dad fixed the tree in the garden with a wooden stake, and this afternoon we helped him tidy up, brushing up lots of leaves from the garden, and outside on the path and road, and putting them in bags. Dad said he's going to make compost from them, like you used to for using in the garden.

Hugo and I kept making big piles of leaves and jumping and running through them. I love the sound of leaves and their colours.

Amy called me and said that when she was sweeping the leaves up in her back garden she found a hedgehog!

It started raining again this evening and everything looked so bare and empty. We had sausages and beans again! Then we lit the fire and just watched TV till bedtime.

I wish you were here.

Love,
Lucie x

Tuesday 25th October

Mum,

I saw you again . . . I was sitting in class and I looked
out the window and there you were, standing near the
school railings in your blue coat, just standing waiting for
me. I wanted to shout and run outside to you, but I knew
that even though she is really nice Mrs Martin wouldn't
have let me.

You just stood there, looking up at the window as if you
could see me too. Your hair was long and glossy again
and you were smiling and happy. I leaned over to wave
at you and you laughed and waved back at me. The
minute the school bell went I grabbed my bag and coat
and ran out to you. Lots of mums and dads were there,
but when I ran to the railings you were gone. I searched
everywhere, but I couldn't see you. Why couldn't you just
wait a few minutes longer for me? Why?

I walked home with Hugo and Conor. I kept hoping that
I'd see you again. I didn't say anything to Hugo because
I didn't want to upset him . . .

Mum, please come back again. I really want to see you.

Please! Please! Please!

Love,
Lucie x

Dear Mum,

Tomorrow is the last day of school before our mid-term break. Roz is going to England for a few days to stay with her sister, and Granny and Granddad are both sick with coughs and colds so Dad has organised for a lady from Moldova to come and look after us while he's at work. Her name is Lara. We all told Dad that we didn't need her, but he said that he can't take any more time off work and that someone has to be here when we're at home during the holiday. Chloe screamed at him and said we don't want a stranger coming to our house, but Dad says he's 'doing what's best for us'.

Chloe says Lara is not allowed in her room or to touch her things. But Hugo and I don't really mind. I hope that she is nice and that she helps with some of the housework too, and that she can cook something other than tacos or soup or something on toast!

I can't believe that it is almost Halloween.

Chloe is going to a big Halloween disco with Tim at the local youth club. I asked Hugo if he wanted to go trick or

treating with me and Amy, but he said that he doesn't
like Halloween any more and he doesn't want to dress up.
He said that he hates witches and ghosts and ghouls and
monsters. Amy and I were going to dress up as witches,
but if Hugo doesn't want to I won't either. Dad said that
maybe the three of us can go to the cinema instead.

  I think Hugo is afraid of Halloween!

Love,
Lucie x

Dear Mum,

Lara was here when we came home from school today. She has blonde hair and is really nice. She is trying to learn English, but gets some of her words mixed up a bit.

She made Hugo and I strip our beds and pick up all the mess from our floors so she could clean both of our bedrooms. She did so much cleaning, she is amazing. Lara said that she loves cleaning things and getting things tidy, which is a good thing as my bedroom had got really messy!

When we'd helped Lara she sent Hugo and me out for a walk. We went down near the park where some older boys are building a big bonfire. When we came home the kitchen was all shiny and bright with no mess.

We had proper home-made chicken and vegetable casserole for dinner.

Lara said Chloe was really pretty and she said she would show her how to colour- code her clothes in the wardrobe.

Lara likes singing along to the radio and watching soap

operas on the TV as they help her to learn English.

I like her and maybe it won't be so bad having her as our minder sometimes.

Love,
Lucie x

Mum,

Hugo had a really bad dream. He came into my bed again. He keeps thinking about zombies and vampires and I told him they are just stories people make up and write about in a book or a film. Then he asked me if I believed in ghosts and I didn't know what to say. I do believe in ghosts and spirits . . . I wanted to tell him about you and how I could see you sometimes, but I didn't want to make him scared again so I didn't say anything.

Hugo misses you so much. I hope he stops having nightmares soon.

Mum, can't you make him have good dreams, not bad ones?

Love,
Lucie xx

Happy Halloween, Mum!

I got Dad to buy a pumpkin and I carved it, the way you used to, and put it out on the doorstep. Then I painted a black cat on the glass door and stuck up two spooky spiders, but Hugo still said he doesn't want to go trick or treating with me. Mark asked him to his house for a Halloween fancy-dress party, but he won't go.

Chloe is the only one in our house who dressed up this year. She went to the disco as a vampire. She put white make-up on her face and wore really heavy black eye make-up. She even had brilliant sharp pointy teeth – she looked really scary! Tim came to pick her up. He was dressed as a werewolf with fangs. Dad took photos of the two of them.

Dad took Hugo and me to the cinema to see a really good film called *The Mad Scientist*. It was so funny we all loved it. We got a milkshake after and then went and watched fireworks up near the green.

Hugo is sleeping on the camp bed in my room tonight as he is scared again. He doesn't need to be scared of you. Even if you are a ghost or spirit I know you would never, ever do anything to hurt him or frighten him.

I'm glad Halloween is over.

Love,
Lucie x

Wednesday 2nd November

Dear Mum,

I went over to Amy's this afternoon. We went to the cinema and then her mum took us for pizza. I had pepperoni.

Today was a good day!

Love,
Lucie x

Chère Maman,

I keep listening to the phone. That way I can hear your voice again and again. I love your accent and sometimes I phone our house number or your mobile number just to hear you talking.

'Hello, this is the Ryans. Sorry we are not able to take your call right now, but please leave your name and number and we will get back to you. Leave your message after the beep.'

I love listening to it over and over. And even though no one really speaks about it, I know that Chloe and Dad do it too, just wanting to hear your voice. It makes us feel you are still at home or at the other end of your mobile somewhere and not very far away.

'Hi, this is Madeleine. Sorry I missed your call, but please leave your name and number and I will call you back.

Thank you.'

I'm never going to let anyone change the phone messages
ever! But I wish you could talk to us . . . Mum, do you
think where you are you can do that?

Please try.

Love,
Lucie x

Dear Mum,

Yesterday I went to Jess's house to have dinner and stay the night. Amy came too but she couldn't stay the night as it was her dad's birthday and they were having a special family dinner.

Jess's mum painted her bedroom and it is really nice now, she says she didn't want it all girly pink with fairies any more. Now it's lilac and white and Jess has photos of horses pinned up all over one wall.

Jess loves horses and now she even goes riding some Saturdays. She said I can come one Saturday morning with her to try it out if Dad lets me. I like horses and ponies, but I'm not sure I want to ride one yet, what do you think?

Jess rides a huge horse called Ginger. She says Ginger is a really good horse, but a bit fast sometimes and she nearly fell off once when he stopped suddenly to chew some grass. I'd hate to fall off a horse.

Her mum made Chicken Provençal for dinner. It was OK,

but not half as nice as yours. I don't think her mum really likes cooking. We watched a few DVDs and had some Nutella and toast before we went to bed.

It was weird being in Jess's bedroom and when I tried to go to sleep I just couldn't. Jess went to sleep straight away, but I tossed and turned. Then I had a bad dream and when I woke up I was crying. I wanted to go home, but Jess was still asleep and it was too late to phone Dad to come and get me as he would be in bed too.

I lay awake for ages. I wanted to feel you around me or near me, but in Jess's room it was all so strange.

I tried reading some of her books. they were mostly about horses and vampires, but I found 'Goodnight Mister Tom' and began to read that.

Then Jess's mum came in to check on us and saw me sitting up. She said if I wanted she'd get dressed and run me back home, but I knew it was too late and I didn't want to wake everyone up.

'Maybe it's a bit too soon for you to stay over? I know Jess really wanted to have you stop over, but Lucie, you probably just need to be around your family at the moment.'

I think she was right. I like going to my friends and I like Jess's house, but I prefer being at home with Hugo and Dad and Chloe, all of us together.

Jess's mum got me a drink of hot chocolate and a biscuit and sat with me for a while and we talked for a bit, and then she made me pull up the quilt and lie down and try to sleep. When I woke up Jess was bouncing on my bed.

After breakfast we played games on Jess's PlayStation until her mum drove me home.

When we got to our house Dad was washing his car and Hugo was helping him and it was so good to be back home again. Chloe was still in bed, but I went upstairs and told her what happened. She said that I'd better not stay at any of my friends' houses for a while. She told me that she'd been invited to a sleepover a couple of weekends ago, but she hadn't gone as she couldn't bear all the girls being happy and chatting and trying to pretend to be normal all night when she felt so awful. She said: 'I can hold it together for a few hours, but not all night long...'

This afternoon we went for a drive round Blessington Lakes

and then had a big walk through the woods. We saw some squirrels and I think I saw a deer in the distance. On the way home we stopped off and got fish and chips.

It's good to be home where I can tell you near me.

I'm so tired tonight, yawn, yawn, yawn.

Love,
Lucie (your sleepyhead) x

ZZZ^z

Hi Mum,

The holidays are over booo . . . hooo . . . hoo! We went back to school today.

Megan's mum had a baby during the holidays. Her new little brother's called Finn. Megan had a photo of him on her phone, he's so cute! He's got black hair and looks a lot like Megan.

Lizzy's granddad is very sick and had to go to hospital. He is ninety which is really old.

Dad has asked Lara to come three afternoons a week to mind us and to help in the house. Granny will still collect me on Wednesdays, but now we only need to go to Roz's on Tuesday after school.

I'm glad that we've got Lara. I like her, and it will be nice to be at home rather than always being at other people's houses or rushing about. I think that even Chloe is getting to like her now.

Dad has started working really late and Lara is going to

stay until he gets home and make us dinner.

Chloe says she thinks Dad doesn't want to come home, that he prefers being in his office to being here with us.

On Friday Hugo is having three friends home after school and Lara says that she will show them how to make pancakes and chocolate sauce.

Love,

Lucie x

Dear Mum,

Today I went swimming with Amy and Jess, it was a lot of fun. But when I got home Dad was up in the bedroom with boxes and bags all over the floor. He had the wardrobe open and was taking out all your clothes and skirts and dresses and shoes and boots.

'Dad, what are you doing?'

'What does it look like?'

I know what it looked like. Dad was getting rid of all your things.

'Dad, stop it! They're Mum's things!' I grabbed some of the clothes, trying to stop him. 'What are you doing with Mum's things? Leave them alone.'

'I have to do this, Lucie. Mum would want me to give her clothes and things to people who will use them instead of just sitting here in the wardrobe and drawers. I have to do this. You know your mum was always giving stuff to the charity shops.'

'that was stuff she didn't want any more!'

'She doesn't need any of these things any more,' he said

firmly. 'they are just hanging there and every time I open the wardrobe door I see them.'

I yelled to Chloe to tell her to come upstairs and see what Dad was doing. I thought she could make him stop because he wouldn't listen to me. When Chloe saw what he was doing she screamed at him to stop. Dad looked like he was going to fight with her, but instead sat down on the bed.

'I can't do this, girls. I'm sorry, but every time I open the wardrobe or pull out a drawer I see her things. Smell her perfume. She's everywhere!'

Chloe and I didn't know what to say. The bedroom is full of your stuff: three-quarters of the wardrobe holds your clothes, the dressing table is still covered with your make-up and perfume and lotions, and the bathroom has your shampoos and shower gel.

None of us knew what to do.

Then Chloe looked at the wardrobe and began to take things out and put them on the bed. 'this can go. This can go. Mum never liked this skirt. Those boots, the heel was too high.'

Dad said nothing and just began to silently put things in the boxes.

'If there is anything you girls want,' he said, looking at the growing pile of clothes and shoes and jackets. 'All your mum's bits and pieces and handbags and belts are yours if you want them. Of course all her good jewellery will be shared between the two of you once you are old enough, it's what mum wanted.'

'Can I keep these three dresses and the skirt Mum got at the market in Paris and her suede jacket?' asked Chloe firmly, grabbing the things she wanted. 'I'll put them in my room.'

I didn't know what I wanted. But Chloe said, 'Lucie should have Mum's red print dress. It's designer and will look better on her when she is older than on me.'

I felt like a pirate on a pirate ship dividing up the treasure they had found in an old sea chest.

'Can I have Mum's dressing gown?' I asked Dad. I know your dressing gown is very old, Mum, but I really want to keep it because it still smells of you and is warm and fluffy.

'Of course,' Dad said, taking it off the hook behind the bedroom door. 'She loved that tatty old dressing gown. I wanted to buy her a new one, but it was her old one she always preferred. . . We can finish this off after tea,' he said, looking at all the mess and boxes. 'Let's get out of the house.'

Then we all went to Eddie Rocket's for hamburgers and chips.

When we got back from dinner Dad went back up to your room and started packing up boxes and labelling them – some to keep, but most to give away to the charity shop. I think he's still up there now, even though we've all gone to bed.

Lying in bed I have your dressing gown over my quilt. It is like a big pink blanket keeping me safe and warm, almost as if you were here sitting on the bed, reading me a story or talking to me. I love to touch it and stroke it and put my cheek and face against it. I love that it smells of you and if I close my eyes I can imagine that it's you sitting with me as I fall asleep.

I love you, Mum.

Love,
Lucie (all snuggy, huggy and warm wrapped up in your old dressing gown) x

14th November

Dear Mum,

The boxes are all gone. Your bedroom feels very strange, but when I went into it today I smelled your favourite French perfume . . . like you had just sprayed it and then left the room, like you had only just been here. I remember that sometimes you gave me a little spray of it too.

I think that it was a sign from you, to show that you are still near even if most of your clothes and stuff gone. I hope that it means you're not angry that we had to give your clothes away.

I love you and I love your perfume.

Love,
Lucie x

Dear Mum,

After school today Chloe, Hugo and I all went to meet a lady called Anna. She's a counsellor who helps kids who have lost a parent or a brother or sister. Roz told Dad about her. We all have to go once a week to visit her and talk about 'how we feel'.

Her office is in Ranelagh in a big old house overlooking the square. She had lots of comfy chairs and cushions and couches and she said we could sit on any chair we liked – we could even lie down on the couch!

Anna told us that her mum died when she was thirteen. Her mum collapsed and had something wrong with her brain. By the time she and her big sister went to the hospital their mum had died. Anna said that it was the worst thing in the world that had ever happened to her but somehow they and their dad got through it.

'You know it wasn't easy to learn to be happy again, but somehow we did,' she said.

After talking to the three of us Anna asked to talk to us all separately. Chloe was first, while Hugo and I played some games on Anna's PlayStation in the other room. Chloe was in with her for ages. Then it was Hugo's turn to go and talk to her and then mine.

Anna asked me a lot about school and my friends and Mrs Martin my teacher. She asked me all about you and the things we did together, the things that made me happy. She asked me how I felt when you got sick and I told her that I felt upset and worried, but everyone said that you were going to get better and I believed that too. We all did. . .

I liked Anna and even though it was difficult to talk to someone I didn't really know it was nice to talk about you and how wonderful you were. Next week we are all coming back to see her again.

Love,
Lucie x

Mum,

I know you were here again tonight.

I could sense you.

You were singing softly. *Blackbird singing. . .*

I could smell you and feel your hair and you touched me.

For a moment it was really lovely to feel that you were close to me again, but then you were gone. . .

Love,

Lucie x

Dear Mum,

Our house is a sad house!

It used to be a happy house with five happy people –
now there are just four of us living in a sad house.

It is two months since you left this world. Sixty-one days
since we said goodbye to you.

We all feel so sad today.

I miss you so much and will love you forever and ever.

Love,

Lucie x

Thanksgiving Day (24th November)

Dear Mum,

Mrs Martin told us all about the pilgrims going to America and settling there and all the other people who left their countries and went to America. Becky's American so tonight her family will celebrate Thanksgiving with a big turkey dinner, like we have at Christmas. Everyone has different traditions. Rama's family don't even have turkey or Christmas at all! Because it's Thanksgiving we all had to think of things we are grateful for. I said that I am grateful for my family and for my friends, and for having Mrs Martin as my teacher.

Chloe wouldn't eat dinner again. Lara made yummy spaghetti Bolognese, but Chloe said she didn't want any of it and just had a slice of toast and cheese. She's so annoying and such a drama queen! I think she must be on a big diet because she won't eat chocolate or sweets any more and just drinks Diet Coke all the time.

After dinner I helped Lara with her English work. She goes to class one night a week in town. Last week she learned twelve new words and I helped her practise using them and writing them down. Lara showed me a photo of her family in Moldova. She has two brothers and a sister and they live on a farm. I think she really misses them, but she has come here to make money and learn English. I'm glad that she's here to take care of us.

Dad came home really late, but even though I was in bed he came in to talk to me and say goodnight. He looked tired, but he said he has to work on a big new project with the rest of the team so he'll be late tomorrow night too.

Love,

Lucie x

Saturday 26th November

Mum,

Some days when I go up to your bedroom I just lie on your bed and pretend that you are still here and have called me to come in and sit down beside you and tell you what I did today in school or with my friends. I lie against the pillows and pretend that you are beside me, talking to me and holding my hand. It's just you and me. No nurses or doctors, no injections or you feeling too sick or tired to speak, just you and I singing songs and talking like we used to. I pull the quilt up and close my eyes and you are there beside me . . . talking and laughing and everything is all right again because you are there.

Tonight I fell asleep on your bed and when I woke up Dad was home from work and was sitting next to me.

I told him that I liked to sit on your bed and pretend. . .

He said, 'No matter how sick your mum was she loved all of you coming into bed beside her and talking to her and being close . . . That's why she didn't want to stay in the hospital when she got really sick; she wanted to be here at home with us all.'

It made me feel sad and happy at the same time to think that you wanted to be with us so much that you came home even though you knew that you wouldn't get better here.

Mum, I wish you were still here at home with us.

When I write to you I feel closer to you. I imagine you reading my letters and words and it makes me feel as if you are still around and near me and knowing what's happening in my life. I love writing letters to you because I can say what I really think and feel and I don't have to keep pretending everything is OK when it isn't and never will be again.

Love,

Lucie (your little letter writer) x

Sunday 27th November

Dear Mum,

The big granite headstone with your name is on top of your grave now. It is rounded like the ones you see sometimes in the park, and we all like the feel of it. It has black writing carved into it with your name:

Madeleine Ryan (nee Aubert)
Beloved wife, mother, daughter and sister,

We put flowers there today and planted two heather plants with purple flowers in the stone flower stand at the base. Then we all said a few prayers for you.

The grass has grown over your grave and you'd like it because it is in a really sunny spot and there is a big tree nearby with lots of red berries. Dad says it is a rowan tree which is one of your favourites.

I still cannot believe that you are lying in a box in the ground under our feet.

Dad says that the body is just a shell, it's the soul and spirit that matter, but having a grave gives us a special place to come and visit and to think of you.

Because it was Sunday there were lots of people visiting their family graves too. There is a little baby called Claire buried on one side of you. She died five months ago. There is a stone teddy and an angel on her grave. On the other side there is an old man called Leo Byrne and his wife Sally. Maybe you will meet them all in heaven!

Graveyards are so quiet and peaceful and some of the graves have big crosses or lots of plants and flowers growing around them. Amy and Jess say they hate graveyards because they are spooky dark places full of ghosts and spirits, but looking around us all the people lying here are part of someone's family . . . just like you. How can you be scared of that?

Chloe said, 'try coming here at night!'

The graveyard doesn't open at night. . .

Hugo got really upset when it was time for us to leave. He said that he didn't want to leave you lying buried deep in the ground in a dark coffin.

'Mum's not there, Hugo. She's not really there,' Dad told

him. 'that's just the old body that Mum doesn't need any more. Do you remember the morning she died? We were all with her and we opened the bedroom window to let her spirit go. . . Don't you remember the sun and the breeze and the sky, and how we all felt it because your mum was free of being sick and sad, and that her spirit was soaring in the sky leaving behind the sick body she didn't need any more. We didn't want her to go, we wanted to keep her with us forever, but Mum had to go because she was too sick to stay with us any longer.'

I could see the tears in his eyes and I had to turn away because I knew I was crying too. 'Mum will always be with you.' He said to us all, 'You don't have to come back to this graveyard if you don't want to. This is a place to mark your mum's passing, a place for everyone to visit, say a prayer and remember her. But if you don't want to come any more you don't have to because we don't need headstones and flowers on a grave to remember her or think of her, because Mum is always with us.'

When we got home Hugo was still upset. Dad says we are not bringing Hugo to your grave again. He says he'll get

Anna to talk to him about it, but please, Mum, can you do anything to help Hugo understand? Why can't you let him know that you're OK, let him see or feel you the way I can?

Love,
Lucie x

30th November

Mum,

I woke up in the middle of the night because I heard a guitar. I ran downstairs, but it was only Dad sitting alone in the study playing it.

I listened for a while. Then Dad saw me and I sat in the armchair while he played for a bit. Dad passed me the guitar and I played a song you showed me and I tried to remember the chords. I loved it when you were teaching me and I still really want to learn to play like you did. I asked Dad if he could teach me but he said he's not good enough. I don't think he wants to. Then he said it was time for me to go back to bed as he had to do some work on his laptop and he put the guitar away.

I wish I could play like you . . . but I don't know how I'll ever learn to play now.

Love,
Lucie x (feeling so sad without you)

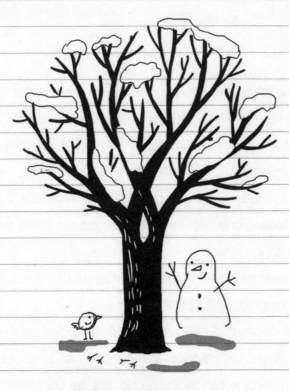

Winter

Mum,

The heating was broken in school. It was *freeeeezzzezing* so Mrs Martin let us wear our coats and jackets in class. Jamie was wearing a funny woollen hat that covers his ears, but Mrs Martin made him take it off.

I hate winter. It's so wet and cold and miserable. If I was a hedgehog or a bear I'd hibernate and not come out till it was spring.

Amy says it's only twenty-four days to Christmas, but I don't want to think about Christmas.

You used to make December special. Today we'd hang up a big Advent calendar in the kitchen and then each take turns to open the doors and find the chocolate surprise until it was Christmas Day. It was the start of having fun and getting ready for Christmas.

But Dad didn't even buy a calendar; he said we don't need one this year!

Today's a grey and sad missing you day.

Love,

Lucie x

Mum,

I saw you in the street today near the library. You were in front of me and I could see you walking along and I began to follow you. I called you, but you didn't look back and kept walking as if you didn't hear me or see me. I wanted you to slow down to wait for me to catch up with you, but you kept walking, moving further away from me.

By the time I turned round the corner of Park Road you were gone. Mum, where did you go? Why didn't you wait for me?

I looked everywhere and ran into all the shops to see if I could find you, talk to you, touch you, but like a cloud you had disappeared.

I saw you. I know I did. Mum, why didn't you wait for me? Stay and talk to me?

I know I saw you. Please come back again.

Love,

Lucie x

Mum,

Are you a ghost?

Sometimes I can see you, hear you, smell you, feel you and sense you really close by me, so close that I could touch you.

I miss you so much.

Love,

Lucie x

PS. I'm not afraid of ghosts

Dear Mum.

What are we going to do about Christmas!

Dad says that he doesn't feel like celebrating Christmas without you. Granny and Granddad want us to have Christmas dinner with them but Dad said no. Roz and Johnny asked us to come in next door to them, and Poppa and Mémé invited us to come to Paris, but Dad said no. He says that he's not going to pretend to be jolly and that it's far better that the four of us stay home and have a quiet Christmas dinner this year and we'll go to Granny's for dinner on St Stephen's Day.

Hugo says that this is going to be the worst Christmas ever . . . no tree, no turkey, no presents, no fun. . . He says Dad is like Mr Scrooge and doesn't want Christmas to happen at all. We always had great Christmases, but this year looks like it is going to be awful, really awful.

Everyone else is excited about Christmas! In school we are collecting toys for presents for children in Africa. I have to get something for a little girl who is about three and put it in a shoebox covered in pink paper. Granny says she'll

take me to the toy shop to buy something nice for the girl
and ask the shoe shop for an empty box.

Mum – please. . . Please make Dad change his mind
about Christmas . . . please. . .

Love,
Lucie x

Mum,

We went to see Anna again. I like going to her as we can talk and say how we feel about everything, and it doesn't matter if we get upset.

Chloe said that she's really angry at you because you wouldn't talk to her properly about your cancer and your treatment. She feels that you didn't trust her or want her to know what the doctors were really saying. Anna told her that you were just trying to protect her, protect all of us, from knowing exactly how sick you were and how bad your cancer really was. Anna said that nobody wants to die and nobody wants to tell the people they love that they are dying.

Hugo said that he feels scared all the time. He's worried that something bad is going to happen to Dad or Chloe or me or even Granny. He's worried that he might start to forget you.

I didn't tell Anna about seeing you, all the time but I told her about being sad and lonely and worried a lot of the time, and even though I'm meant to be concentrating in school or doing something I always feel you are in my mind. I can't stop thinking about it all. It's like a big heavy rock inside me.

Anna says it's important for us not to hide how we are feeling about things. That's why we come to see her. She's here to listen and to help us to cope with what has happened. At first I didn't want to tell her anything, but now I think that talking to Anna is helping.

Dad has started going to a group set up for people who have lost their husband or wife. It's called the Umbrella Club and they meet once a week in town.
Granny says it's doing Dad good to have other people to talk to who have gone through the same thing, losing the person they love.

Mum, I wish you hadn't died and I wish I wasn't so sad. Anna says we have to try to remember all the good happy times, the years we had when you were well and strong and we had fun just doing ordinary things, and not just remember the bad times, the last few months and weeks when you were so sick.

I am trying.

Love,
Lucie x

Saturday 10th December

Dear Mum,

Auntie Trish took Chloe and me to the hairdresser's to get our hair cut. My hair is so long it keeps getting tangled.

It's weird having someone else cut my hair! When you cut my hair with your special set of scissors and combs and hair clips it was fun! We'd pretend our kitchen was a real hairdressers and you used to ask me silly questions like where I was going on holiday, or whether I had any big plans for the weekend; while I stood in my pyjamas and you'd cut and snip my hair till the floor would be covered with my wet little rat tails. . .

I don't like getting my hair cut now but when it was blow-dried it looked OK, though I think it's too short. Auntie Trish got some highlights in her hair and Chloe got some layers cut near the front of hers. They look kind of cool. Chloe liked the hairdresser's, but I preferred you doing it.

Chloe is going to the cinema tonight again with Tim and is wearing her new pair of jeans.

She's got so skinny her old ones don't fit her any more.

Hugo's gone to Jonathan's birthday party so it will just be me and Dad for dinner tonight. Dad is working in the study as usual and I'm busy writing this let—

I had to stop writing because Chloe just came in to borrow my pencil sharpener for her eyeliner pencil. She asked me what I was writing.

'It's just a letter,' I told her. 'I like writing letters.'

'Who is it to?' she kept on.

'Mum.'

'You are writing to Mum? Do you really think that she can read letters where she is?'

'Yes, I do and besides, I like writing them. It helps.'

'What do you do with them? Do you send them to her?'

'I posted a few . . . but mostly I just write to her and keep them. . . I know Mum is in heaven, but she can still read them and see them!'

'Lucie, you're mad!' she said and took the sharpener back to her room.

I don't care what Chloe says, I like writing letters and I know you like letters too. You told me when you were younger you loved writing them. Emails and texts are great, but they are too short. A letter can say so much more.

I remember when you showed me all the letter stuff you kept in your desk. You let me use your special letter paper and your black ink pen, and then let me read some of the letters that you and Dad wrote to each other when you were first seeing each other, and he was here and you were in France. Now you are gone away again and I am writing to you just like he used to.

I hope that you like reading my letters as much as you liked getting letters from Dad!

Love (and scribbles and hugs),
Lucie x

Mum,

When I went into the kitchen this evening I could sense you nearby. I turned around and you were standing at the cooker. I wanted to touch you, but the minute I said 'Mum' you disappeared!

Then I saw your recipe book. It was on the kitchen table.

You loved that book full of all your favourite recipes. I don't know how it ended up on the kitchen table, but when I opened it I found your recipe for cupcakes. I loved it when we made cupcakes together, and I knew right then that you wanted me to make them.

I asked Dad if it was OK for me to make them on my own and he said fine it I was very careful of the oven.

When I got out all the ingredients and the big mixing bowl it made me think of all the fun we used to have making them. . . In a way I felt like you were there in the kitchen with me too, helping me like you used to.

The smell of the cupcakes baking in the oven made Dad and Hugo and Chloe come into the kitchen, because the smell reminded them of you too. The cupcakes turned out perfect and we all iced them together, using lots of sprinkles and different coloured icing, the way we used to.

Then we all sat down and ate every one of them. Even Chloe had two. We sat in the kitchen for ages talking about all the things you used to cook and the time you made a hundred cupcakes for our school fair and wouldn't let us eat any as they were for charity, but made us some more yummy ones the next day that were just for us!

Love,
Lucie (your *petite chef*) x

The Best Cupcakes in the World

Ingredients:

2 eggs

125 grams softened butter

125 grams caster sugar

150 grams flour

For icing:

75 grams softened butter

125 grams icing sugar

Method:

Preheat oven to 190c

Put cupcake cases on a baking tray or very lightly butter each little cupcake tin holder. Cream the butter in a big bowl until it begins to soften a bit and add sugar and mix until light and fluffy. Add two eggs and mix all together. Sift in flour and beat the mixture with an electric mixer. Spoon the mixture into your cases or cupcake tins. Put in oven and cook for about 8 - 12 minutes. Leave to cool before icing and decorating.

For icing:

Cream butter and icing sugar together. Spread on top of each cupcake.

Dear Mum

Yesterday we all brought our shoeboxes to school. I got my little girl a cute doll with long hair that you can plait, and a brush, and some colouring pencils and a colouring book, and a ball and a *Peppa Pig* book. I hope she likes them.

Hugo is a shepherd in his class play and Chloe's school are doing a sponsored fast next week and Chloe cannot eat anything for twenty-four hours. That's easy peasy for her as most days she hardly eats anyway. She is only allowed drinks and thin soup. All the money they collect will go to help people who are starving in Somalia and Ethiopia.

Even though everyone keeps going on about Christmas it still doesn't feel like Christmas. Dad is being really strange and won't talk about it, as if he hopes it will just go away.

Today Chloe told him that we have to put up a Christmas tree.

'Not this year.' he said. 'We don't have to do it this year. People will understand.'

But Hugo doesn't understand and he got so upset that Dad had to promise to bring him to pick a Christmas tree at the weekend.

Chloe told Dad that he was being unfair and that we couldn't just ignore Christmas. She told him that he has to go to the big supermarket and order a Christmas turkey special food package for us. She said that she and I would cook it together and see if we can find Mum's special stuffing recipe in the book.

Then she told him that she was going to take me shopping on Saturday to get some presents for everyone as we have to have some to put under the tree. Dad just nodded and said OK. We couldn't believe it!

Thanks, Mum.

Love,

Lucie x

P.S. Next Monday we start our Christmas tests. Mrs Martin says we have to revise all the things we learned this term if we want to do well. How can I do well when some days I can't even think!

Dear Mum,

  While Dad was doing the shopping this evening I called in
to the bookshop to see Mr Humphrey. They were open late
and all their Christmas books are in the window and on red-
coloured tables everywhere. A new lady called Kim is working
there now. She has black hair with pink tips and really big
earrings and was super nice to me. Tess gave me a big hug
and said how much they'd missed me calling into the shop.
She got a new black kitten called Tilly six weeks ago.

  Mr Humphrey showed me some of the new children's books
and told me to browse and pick one out for myself.

  'I can't do that, Mr Humphrey,' I said. I hadn't got enough
money with me to buy a book.

  'Lucie, you pick out whatever book you want and it's yours.
Maybe you can write me a short review and I can put it up
in the children's section so kids will know that another kid
recommended it. Your mum always wrote wonderful reviews.
Customers would go by what Madeleine recommended to
read.'

  It took ages as there were so many books I wanted, but

eventually I picked one. It's about a brother and sister who get trapped in a storm and no one knows where they are and they have to try to survive it. It's called 'Storm'. Mr Humphrey said it was a good choice.

'I'll write the review as soon as I've finished it,' I promised.

Above his counter Mr Humphrey has the big staff photo with you all holding a big pile of your favourite books in your arms. It reminded me how much you loved working here and how much you loved reading, just like me.

Mr Humphrey noticed me looking at the picture and said, 'Lucie, I hope you know that you are always welcome here. Those of us who need to be around stories and words and books are a very special breed. Even though your mum isn't here any more I hope you still feel at home coming to visit us here in the shop. . . Your mum would want that.'

Mr Humphrey is so nice and like you I love his shop.

Love,
Lucie (your little bookworm) x

P.S. Storm is brilliant.

Dear Mum,

Chloe is driving me mad. All she does is talk about Tim! She is an utter pain!

I asked her to help me study for my maths test, but she wouldn't cos she's too busy!!!!

She's so mean and doesn't want to hear about anything except for Tim . . . *grrr*. . . All she talks about is Tim. . . What a great boyfriend he is. . . What she and Tim are going to do. . . What Tim said. . . What she will get Tim for Christmas!

When she grows up she says they are going to get married . . . YUK YUK YUK! Then she'll be Mrs Chloe Frost. Hugo calls her 'Mrs Frosty the Snowman' which makes her mad.

I guess Tim is OK, but why Chloe likes him so much I don't know. He's got spots on his chin and on his neck and is only a bit taller than her. His hair is greasy too and he spends most of his time on his iPhone when he is over here. Now Chloe wants Dad to get her one too.

Dad says not to mind her and that we shouldn't bank on Chloe becoming Mrs Frosty. He says that Chloe is just 'infatuated' at the moment, but that she won't be forever.

I do miss being with Chloe because now she wants to spend all her spare time with Tim and not go anywhere with us.

They usually hang out in Dundrum shopping centre (boring) or go to the cinema or to Eddie Rocket's. She won't come swimming with us or go bowling or do any family things if Tim is around.

Tonight Dad said Chloe couldn't go out with Tim as they'd been together most of the day and he was going to the pub for a pint with Johnny and Roz, so he wanted her to mind Hugo and me.

Chloe got really cross and told him that he was horrible and mean, and that if you were here you would not stand in her way and would know all about boyfriends and what a girl her age feels.

Dad said that he might not know what a girl her age feels or thinks, but he has a very good idea about hormones and what teenage boys think.

I hope that Hugo doesn't get spots like Tim when he's a teenager.

Chloe is mad with us now and is in her room phoning and texting everyone about how mean Dad is. I told her that even if you were here you still wouldn't let her go out tonight, but she didn't like that very much and screamed at me to get out of her room and never come back into it. Never, ever ... ever. I am banned from it.

She is being an awful big sister at the moment. I wish that Tim would go away.

Love,

Lucie x

P.S. Mum if I fail my maths test tomorrow it's partly Chloe's fault, Please make it easy . . . please.

P.P.S. I think I am going to fail.

Mum,

Hurray! We got our Christmas tree. It's not as big as usual, but it's so fresh it makes the house smell of pine. The top is a bit wonky, but Dad says it's fine.

He got the lights and decorations from the attic and we decorated it and now it looks all twinkly with stars and red bows. Then we hung up all our stockings in the hall, yours too!

When we'd finished decorating, Dad went off to work in his study and let us put up the nativity scene, with its figures of Mary and Joseph and baby Jesus and the santons, you bought in the Christmas market in Paris when you got married. We got moss and ivy and branches from the garden to decorate it. Then we put the silver reindeers inside our front door and hung the big swag over the fireplace. We found the CD of Christmas songs that you always played around the house and put it on. It felt good listening to 'Rudolph the Red- nosed Reindeer', 'Let it snow', and 'We wish you a Merry Christmas'. Hugo and I tried to pretend you were here with us too.

Afterwards we just sat around the fire and Chloe made popcorn. We were all thinking about last year before you got really sick and everyone was together and happy. We never guessed that it would be our last Christmas ever with you. . .

I wish that you could see the tree and the stockings and everything.

Mum, why can't you be here for Christmas?

Love, (and hugs)
Lucie x

19th December

Good Night Mum.

It's so dark outside but when I look at the moon and stars outside I think of you.

Twinkle . . . Twinkle . . . little Star

Love,

Lucie x

Mum,

Why did you have to die?

Losing you is the VERY worst thing that could happen to me and to Dad and Chloe and Hugo!

Why did God pick you to die?

Granny says that sometimes 'bad things happen to good people' and that even if we don't understand why we must try to accept it.

I don't want to accept it! I want you to come back!

Why did you leave us?

Love,
Lucie x

Mum,

Yippee! Today was the last day of school! Mrs Martin said that I have done very well in my tests. She said this year may be a strange Christmas without you, but to remember that we are together, and that Christmas is all about family.

Hugo's play went really well and we are all so proud of him. You would have been too. He was a great shepherd and his class sang 'Little Donkey' and he sang a bit on his own!

Chloe had fun doing her fast, her whole class slept all night in sleeping bags in their school hall. They raised lots of money for Africa but she was so tired after.

Lara is going to Moldova on Friday for twelve days to see her family. Dad will be on holiday so he can mind us.

I can't believe that Christmas is only four days away.

Love,
Lucie x

Saturday 24th December

Dear Mum,

It's Christmas Eve. Dad took us into Grafton Street this morning to have a look around and do some last-minute shopping. We got some lovely perfume for Granny and Dad got Granddad a cashmere jumper, as he always has ancient old ones and really needs a new one.

It's really cold and frosty outside, but it's lovely to see all the Christmas trees and their lights and decorations in people's windows. The Andersons have the biggest tree as usual, and have put a big Santa with coloured lights and a sleigh up on their lawn.

Tonight we went to midnight mass. The church was really crowded! All the neighbours were there: Roz and Johnny and the boys, the Andersons and the O'Gradys' with their daughter Nicola and her family who are home from New York. Amy and her family were there and Mr Humphrey and his mother were there too.

Father Lennon said a special prayer for all the family members that are missing this year. The church was covered in candles and they were all shimmering in the dark. It felt so magical that it made me wonder if you were there too. . . Afterwards everyone stood around wishing everyone Happy Christmas. I love midnight mass.

When we got home we had hot chocolate and some toast before we went to bed.

I know that all of us were feeling sad and thinking about you, but none of us want to say it and spoil things.

I wish you were here for Christmas, Mum, I really do.

Love,
Lucie x

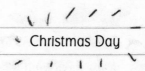

Happy Christmas, Mum!

I can't believe that it's Christmas. There were Santa presents for us all under the tree! I got a guitar and a songbook! Imagine a guitar of my own! Dad says that I can start guitar lessons after Christmas. I am going to try and learn to play. Dad has your old song notebooks and some beginner guitar books. I am going to practise and practise before I begin my proper lessons. Dad said that when the two of you got married you showed him how to play your guitar.

'She was the musician in the family! I'm afraid I'm not half as good as your mother was.'

Getting a guitar of my own and going to proper music lessons is the best Christmas present ever! Chloe doesn't like the guitar and Hugo says when he is older he wants to play the drums! But I want to be just like you, Mum.

Hugo got a massive Transformer set and Chloe got a big make-up kit and a pair of grey boots, which are really cool. We got a book each and a big chocolate selection box too.

After we'd opened our presents we went to take some red

Christmas flowers to your grave. There were lots of people up at the graveyard even though it was very cold and windy.

When we got home Roz asked us all to come in for a drink next door. Dad and Chloe wouldn't come, but Hugo and I did. Killian and Conor got a new PlayStation and some games. Conor got a Transformer too. All their family were there so we didn't stay too long.

Chloe and Dad and I all cooked the dinner. The turkey breast was in a silver tray ready to put in the oven and there were roast potatoes and vegetables and stuffing, and even a special dish with the gravy in. When it was cooked it all turned out OK, but it wasn't a special Christmas dinner like you cooked last year. It made me miss you even more . . . nothing is the same without you.

We ate in the dining room which was a bit weird when there are only four of us. Dad forgot to get Christmas crackers so we played a game pretending that we had some. Afterwards we had *Bûche de Noël* and ice cream.

Then Dad gave us his presents. We each got a phone! Dad said that we are to always keep our phones with us and he'd already put his number in them so we can call him whenever we need him.

Chloe and I got a pair of silver earrings too. Mine have wings on them! Hugo got a football game for the Wii.

I got Chloe a CD she really wanted and blue nail polish and she gave me a cool pink jewellery box with my initial on it, and Hugo got me a pair of slippers that are all fluffy like a dog. They are so comfy. I got him a Spiderman figure and a set of Spiderman cards.

We got Dad a big photo album with photos of all of us in it and we framed that big picture Uncle Theo took of us on the beach in France two years ago. Dad said that he loved his presents, but I could tell it made him sad to see the picture where we were all so happy. We all had a bit of a cry when we put the family photo up on the big dresser. We got him a pair of cuff links that say 'Best Dad' too.

'Well, you lot are the best kids ever,' Dad said, hugging us all.

I don't know what you do in heaven to celebrate Christmas, but *Joyeux Noel!*

Love,
Lucie x

Dear Mum,

Yesterday we went to Granny and Granddad's.

We had turkey and ham and lots of Granny's special roast potatoes. There was so much food that it was like having Christmas dinner all over again.

We got more presents. Granny and Granddad gave me a pink fleece jacket and a silver charm bracelet with two charms, a bird and an angel. I really love it. Granny loved the perfume and Granddad put on his new jumper.

After dinner we played charades and Chloe and Granddad won. We stayed till nearly midnight.

This afternoon I went ice skating with Amy and her two brothers. Her mum drove us into town to Smithfield to the big open-air Christmas ice rink. It's really hard to skate and I was so wobbly that I kept slipping. Amy and I were laughing so much that we kept falling, but then we got the hang of it. Her older brother Jack was brilliant at it and showed us how to stay up and move our skates, but little

Tommy was even worse than us and kept tumbling.

Afterwards I went back to Amy's for tea and her mum said that she would take us all skating again next weekend if we liked – which we really did! Amy asked if I could stay over afterwards and I said that I would.

Love,
Lucie x

P.S. I am reading 'The Little Prince'. Mémé sent it to me for Christmas and said it was your favourite book. I love it too.

New Year's Day

Dear Mum,

Happy New Year!

Well, that's what everyone keeps saying and wishing us, everyone telling us that things will be better for us this year. What they really mean is that things couldn't possibly be worse than they were this year with you dying.

Roz and Johnny had a New Year's Eve party and asked a few of the neighbours around, but Dad said we couldn't go as it wasn't really appropriate. We could hear loud music playing, and laughing from their house and it sounded like everyone was having a good time.

Dad could tell we were sad about missing the party next door so he ordered a huge buffet platter Chinese takeaway with all kinds of things like ribs and wontons and prawn crackers. We all tried everything and then we watched TV, but even on the TV programmes everyone seemed to be having a good time which kind of made it even worse!

Dad made us all wish things for the New Year.

I wished that I could learn to play my new guitar and that would we go to France this summer.

Chloe wished that she and Tim would still be going out by the time Valentine's Day comes. It's important to have a boyfriend for Valentines she says when you are her age.

Hugo said that since we didn't get a dog for Christmas, he wished that we could get a dog for the New Year. Dad said that no matter how much he wishes it we are not getting one. It is only an 'extra responsibility', another thing to feed and be looked after and worry about. He told Hugo to think of something else, but he got upset and wouldn't make another wish!

Dad said he wished that we would all pull together as a family and be strong and help each other. I think we are all doing that already. Wishes! Wishes! Wishes!

I think we all secretly had the exact same wish that you could be here with us. . .

Bonne année!

Love,

Lucie x

Tuesday 3rd January

Dear Mum,

Dad took Hugo and me and Amy and Mark to Funderland today. It was really crowded and I met a few people from school. Amy and I went on the big wheel. It was brill but really scary and we both closed our eyes up on top and then when we opened them we could see all over the city. It was wow!

Hugo and Mark and Dad kept going on the dodgems and trying to crash into us.

The only thing I hated was the ghost train . . . it was so scary I am never going on one of them ever again. Amy and I just screamed and screamed as loud as we could as it was so horrible and creepy.

Afterwards we went for hot dogs and chips.

It was a fun day and it was nice to see Dad having fun too. The only thing that could have made it better would have been if you were there with us.

Love,
Lucie x

4th January

Mum,

  Last night I had a dream about you. I dreamed that you were calling me and calling me and I couldn't find you. I looked everywhere, but I couldn't find you.

  When I woke up Chloe was in my room. She said she'd heard me calling out for you. I was really upset so she stayed talking to me for ages.

Was it a dream or real, Mum?

Love,
Lucie x

Monday 9th January

Dear Mum,

We're back in school and I suppose it's OK. I stayed at Amy's house on Saturday and we went skating again, but I didn't fall half as much this time. The ice rink is closing down soon so I guess we'll have to find somewhere else to practise.

Mrs Martin is teaching us all about the Titanic in history this term. It's hard to believe that such a big ship would sink after hitting an iceberg on its very first journey to America. We have to write a story about it and pretend we are one of the people on the boat.

I looked up some stuff on the internet and there is so much about it. After school I went to the library with Amy and her mum and we both got some books out. Amy is going to write as if she is a really rich lady on the boat. I don't know who I want to be yet.

Natalie invited me to her birthday party the weekend after next. She's asked seven of us and we are going to a pottery studio where you make something from clay and then paint it. Her auntie works there and afterwards we are going back to her house for pizza and cake.

Tomorrow Dad is taking us all to the dentist after school. Yuk, yuk, yuk! I hate going to the dentist! Please make it that I don't need any fillings, please!

Love you and wish you were here to take us to the dentist.

Love,
Lucie x

Mum,

Chloe has to get braces, top and bottom, and she is going crazy. She cried the whole way home in the car and Dad nearly crashed into an old lady crossing the road with her dog, as he was so busy trying to calm her down.

The dentist said that she has too many teeth and they are growing crooked and on top of each other. She has to get a tooth taken out and then get the braces. She doesn't want to get them, but Dad says she has no choice. He said that you would kill him if he didn't make Chloe get braces. It's going to cost a fortune, but Dad says Chloe will thank him when she is older and has a perfect smile.

When we got home Chloe went and stayed in her room and wouldn't come down. I think she's worried that Tim won't like her any more if she has braces . . . Poor Chloe!

My teeth were perfecto! Thanks for making sure I didn't have to have any fillings!

Love,

Lucie (your sparkling-clean-teeth-smiley daughter) x

Dear Mum,

Today I had my first guitar lesson after school. My teacher is called Mr Handford. He's really tall, with long hair and a beard, and he's really nice. I think you would like him.

'Why do you want to play the guitar, Lucie?' he asked me. I didn't even have to think about why.

'My mum and dad both play the guitar. My mum really loved it and I want to be just like her and be able to play and sing and write songs too.'

'Music is in your family, that's good,' he said. 'Lots of kids only want to learn to play guitar so they can be famous, which is the wrong reason! It is all about the music in this room: playing it, learning about it, practising, experimenting and discovering what music can do. Music is constantly changing.'

Mr Handford checked my new guitar and tuned it and then showed me how to play some chords. He was surprised that I knew a few already and could play a little bit. I told him that you showed me.

He made me get out a notebook and draw out the different chords, and gave me some music pages and we played a bit of a song together. It sounded good and I did my best to keep up with him. He asked me if there were any songs that I really wanted to learn to play, and I said I'd like to play 'Blackbird' because it's your favourite.

The lesson lasted for an hour and I couldn't believe it when Mr Handford said our time was up and that he'd see me next week.

I'm going to make sure that I practise every day. Dad said he would try and help me. He's good at the guitar, but not as good as you.

Love,
Lucie x

Dear Mum,

We had to hand in our essays on the Titanic today. Mine is about a girl called Mary who was going to America with her family because they had no money, and couldn't even pay their rent any more. Her uncle lived in New York and he was going to meet them and help them find a new place to live, and get her dad a job. They were all asleep when the iceberg hit, but Mary and her little sister ran as fast as they could to make it up to the deck and on to the lifeboat. They are the only two in the family who survive.

Mrs Martin said my story was excellent with lots of historical research and gave me a gold star.

Me, Chloe and Hugo went to Auntie Trish's for dinner tonight as Dad had to go to a big work thing. We had lasagne and garlic bread.

Love,
Lucie x

Mum,

Chloe got her train tracks today. They are meant to be invisible, but you can still see them. Dad said if Hugo or I make fun of her we are in big trouble.

Chloe can hardly talk and we have to really listen to understand what she is saying; it's as if she has something stuffed in her mouth. She can't eat properly and just wants cool drinks. She said it really hurt when she had them put on and she has to go back next week and get them tightened even more. Poor Chloe . . . I know she is really annoying, but this is awful for her. She says she is not going to school tomorrow and she even turned off her mobile so Tim couldn't phone her, and told us to say that she was out if any of her friends called.

Mum, can you try to make Chloe's mouth feel a bit better and take the pain away. She told Dad to leave her alone. She just wants you. Please, Mum . . . she hates her braces and really needs you.

Love,
Lucie xx

Mum,

Chloe can still hardly eat, but she can talk again. She sounds a bit funny when she talks, but I've got used to it now.

I've been practising the guitar lots and now I can play a bit of 'Delilah' and some of the chords for 'Blackbird'.
Dad is helping me and when I am playing I think of you. I pretend you are sitting beside me listening.

I went to Natalie's 'Pottery Party' yesterday and it was so funny using the wheel as the clay went everywhere and it was so messy. I made a bowl and a plate. We had to paint and decorate them and then leave them so they can fire them in the kiln. Natalie will get them for us next week.

Granddad has to go into hospital to get a new hip. He will be there for a week and then go to a nursing home for a week to rest. He won't be able to walk or drive or play golf for weeks. Granny says that he'll drive her mad, but he needs to get it done.

The weather is getting much colder. I am putting lots of crumbs and some nuts out for the birds and making sure they have water as sometimes the water is frozen in the morning. Today there were two robins looking in the window at me. I think they are the same robins we used to feed last year. Do you remember that we called them Millie and Billy?

I wish you were here so I could talk to you instead of writing to you.

Love,
Lucie x

24th January

Mum,

Last night I heard you singing softly in my room and guitar playing, even though my guitar was downstairs. I sang too. Did you hear me?

Love,
Lucie x

Mum,

Hugo is worried about his birthday on Saturday because you won't be here. He's going to be nine and he has no mother . . . it's not fair! Dad and Chloe and I are doing our best, but we are not you and you are the person he wants the most in the world!

Last night when he was in his pyjamas and going to bed he kept asking me:

'Where is Mummy? When will I see her again?'

I told him you are always around him, watching over him and caring for him. But he was so upset that you left him. I told him that you were very sick and that the medicines didn't work any more and you just kept getting sicker and sicker till your heart stopped working.

'Sometimes I'm frightened that I'll forget her . . . stop remembering her and then she'll stop remembering me,' he said and I felt awful for him.

I told him that will never happen . . . never . . . never . . . never.

I was trying to calm him down by reading a story from his book of Greek legends when Dad came in. He said that he'd finish the story. Dad says Hugo is like a little Greek hero, brave and strong and true.

I like to watch when Dad and Hugo are so close and I'm glad for Hugo because he needs Dad and sometimes Dad needs him too.

Love,
Lucie x

Saturday 28th January

Mum,

It's Hugo's birthday!! We all tried not to be sad about you not being here with us this morning singing 'Happy Birthday' and 'Bon Anniversaire'.

You used to give us birthday hugs and tickles and make French toast and tell us a big long story about the day we were born, so today was different and very hard, especially for Hugo.

Dad bought Hugo a new football kit and football boots and two games for the PlayStation. Chloe and I gave him a big silver Transformer. When Hugo had opened his presents from us Dad gave him the big box wrapped in the blue and silver star paper. Your present. He told Hugo it was from you and that you had chosen it specially for him. Hugo was extra careful opening it and he couldn't believe it when he saw the beautiful globe.

Hugo loves it and went straight upstairs and put it on the shelf beside his bed. There is a light inside it and it really glows and will light up his room so it won't be too dark and scary any more. How did you know the perfect thing to buy for him?

Granny and Granddad and Auntie Trish and Uncle Alan came over to have breakfast with us. Dad made bacon and sausages and toast for everyone.

After lunch we went to the sports centre for Hugo's party. Chloe and I watched the boys play football and played a bit too. Then we tried the climbing wall. It's so high that Chloe got dizzy, but I got about halfway up. Hugo is so light and fast he got all the way to the top and wasn't even scared!

Afterwards everyone went to Rocco's for pizza and there was a big ice-cream cake with nine candles. Chloe only took a small bit of pizza and wouldn't eat any cake . . . she's still on her stupid diet! Hugo was joking and happy with all his friends and I was really glad to see him having such a good time.

I wish you were here today, Mum, but maybe you were.

Love,
Lucie x

Dear Mum,

It snowed today! The snow began to fall like white feathers from the sky while we were in school. Everyone kept looking out of the window, as it was getting heavier and heavier. It covered the schoolyard and the roof and it just kept coming.

Mrs Martin got really cross as no one was listening to her and we just wanted to be outside in the snow instead of learning about boring old fractions. By the time class finished everywhere was white.

Finally the bell rang and we could escape. Everyone was throwing snow and trying to make snowballs. Hugo and I couldn't believe it and kept chasing each other the whole way home.

As soon as we got to the house we wanted to just dump our school bags and get changed so we could play out on our road with all the rest of the kids. Lara made us put on our woollen gloves and hats and scarves and heavy boots.

'OK, homework later. Go out and play snowballs with your friends, but no snowy boots in the house!' she said.

Everyone was out in the road and we had the biggest snowball fight ever. It was mega. When Chloe and a few of the girls from her school came along we all pelted them. Chloe was mad at us.

She changed and came out and pulverised Killian as he kept chasing Hugo. It was great! When Dad came home from work he came out in the snow too, and so did Roz and Johnny. You should have seen them. We had a mega snowball fight, us against the Kellys, and we won! We were all cold and wet when we called a truce and my fingers were so cold I felt like I had frostbite. Dad made us all have a warm shower and we had pork chops for tea.

I LOVE the snow!

I love you too.

Love,
Lucie x

Mum,

It snowed again during the night. It's freezing cold and everywhere is white and totally covered with snow. The driveway, our road and everywhere is white and the cars cannot turn up the hill to get into Rivercourt. Mrs O'Shea's car went into a skid when she tried to get up from the shops last night so she had to leave it and walk all the way back, carrying food for the dinner.

Dad put on the radio to listen to the news as some of the roads are very bad and some schools are shut and the airport is closed for a few hours. The school sent a text to all the parents to say it is closed . . . so we got to stay home and play.

Dad phoned the office and told them that he would have to work from home.

Hugo and I got up early and went outside and made a massive snowman.

Everyone from our street came out in the snow and later

we had the biggest snow battle ever.

I asked Chloe to be on our team, but she just stayed inside in her dressing gown watching TV and phoning people nearly all day.

She is becoming such a nerd now, always on Facebook and texting and never doing anything real like going out in the snow and cold like us.

Dad made a big pot of soup for lunch by mixing two cans together and it was great. He called it *tomato-tail!* We had it with lots of toast.

The garden is covered in snow and it's so deep the birds cannot get worms or insects, and even the trees and plants are covered so there is nothing for them to eat or drink.

I put out lots of food and water for the birds and found some sunflower seeds we keep for salads and put them and some bird peanuts in the green bird feeder. The robins are back, along with some blue tits and two blackbirds and a magpie. He was clever and greedy and kept trying to open the feeder. You always used to feed the birds so that is now my job. Chloe doesn't like birds much, but I do. Sometimes I'd like to be a bird and be able to fly and be free, but on snowy days I'm glad I'm not.

Hugo and I hope the snow lasts and that we get to stay at home and have fun.

Snowy dreams.

Love,
Lucie x

Dear Mum,

When I looked out the window early this morning the snow was white and fresh but there were new footprints all across the back garden.

Nobody was up and the back gate was locked, but someone had walked around the garden.

Was it you coming to see us?

I hope you liked our snowman.

Love,

Lucie x

Dear Mum,

School opened again today. It's sunny and the snow started to melt. It began really slow, first coming off the trees and branches and then where the sun shone on the grass, and then it began falling off the roof.

By the time I got home everything was beginning to get slushy. Our snowman is a small heap on the grass and the igloo that the boys built next door is disappearing bit by bit.

Everything looks dirty and grey and slushy now and you just want it to go away. Chloe says she's glad the snow is gone as we can all get back to normal now!

Love,

Lucie x

P.S. Is there snow in heaven or is the weather always perfect?

Dear Mum,

Today I made Valentine biscuits for everyone.

Chloe was out and Hugo was next door playing with the boys. I finished all my homework and was so bored. I asked Dad if I could do some baking and he said that it was fine as long as I cleaned up the mess in the kitchen and was careful.

I got out your recipe book and looked through all your recipes for the different biscuits you used to make, and then found your special Valentine biscuits! I found the heart-shaped cookie cutters in the top press.

I love baking and making things and these biscuits were so easy-peasy.

When they came out of the oven I tried a biscuit and they had turned out *perfectly!* I'm going to give some to everyone tomorrow.

I found red card in the bottom drawer and I cut it into heart shapes too and put a big heart and a little heart biscuit on top and covered it in cling film.

Reading your recipes and sitting in the kitchen with the oven on makes me remember all the times we came home from school and you baked and made stuff for us. Cooking reminds me of you.

Love (and hearts),
Lucie x

Valentine Biscuits

Ingredients

175 grams plain flour
100 grams butter, softened
50 grams caster sugar
50 grams icing sugar

Method

Preheat oven to 180 C
Put flour in a mixing bowl and
rub in the butter with your fingers.
Add the caster sugar and mix it all together
to make a stiff dough.
Roll out the dough (about ½ cm thick)
and then cut carefully with heart-shaped
cookie cutters and put biscuits on a baking
tray. Cook for 6-10 minutes until they
are a light golden colour.

When the biscuits are cool put a little icing
on top or dust them with icing sugar.

14th February

Happy Valentine's Day Mum!

It is the day to tell the person you love just how much you love them, so I'm telling you.

Chloe and I felt really bad for Dad because we knew he'd miss you lots today, so we made him a card to say we love him because he is the best dad in the world and gave it to him at breakfast. I gave Hugo, Chloe and Dad my biscuits too and they all loved them!
I took some to school too and gave them to people in my class and to Mrs Martin.

Miss Delaney who teaches sixth class got a special delivery of a massive bunch of flowers and five heart balloons. Everyone was trying to look into her classroom to see them. She is the prettiest teacher in school by far. I bet nobody gave grumpy Mrs Edmond flowers or cards. She's a dragon.

When we got home from school Chloe was annoyed because there was no card for her. Maybe Tim has forgotten it's Valentine's Day!

Dad said that instead of going out for Valentine's we were getting a takeaway from Bombay Pantry and we could all order what we wanted. Chloe said she wasn't hungry. She's never hungry nowadays. She eats hardly anything and is so skinny she had to get two new pairs of jeans, but Dad still ordered chicken tikka masala for her and naan bread.

We were just finishing eating when Tim called to the house. He had a big card for Chloe and a bunch of red tulips. Chloe was so happy, it was really sweet!

Dad had got chocolate cake for dessert and Chloe and Tim had some too.

When Tim had gone home Chloe said that Valentine's Day is the best day in the world and that Tim is the best boyfriend!

Chloe is so lucky. I don't think I will ever have a boyfriend or fall in love like you and Dad, or Chloe and Tim, or Miss Delaney and her boyfriend.

Valentine's Day is a lonely day if you are on your own. I hope that you are not too lonely today. We love you.

Love,
Lucie x

Dear Mum,

  When Dad got home from work he got out his guitar and asked me to show him what I'd learned in my lesson today. Dad never had proper guitar lessons so I showed him what Mr Handford made me write down and the sheets he gave me. Dad seemed really happy to see me enjoying learning to play.

  'Your mum loved music, Lucie. I think that you have inherited that from her.'

  When I play the guitar or listen to it I forget things around me and think of what I am playing or hearing. I love music, but I think Dad is wrong. I think I have inherited it from both you and him. It's nice to have something special for me and Dad to share; learning to play the guitar is one of the best things ever!

Love,
Lucie x

Dear Mum,

Granddad had his operation last week to get his new hip.
We weren't allowed to see him when he was in hospital,
but now he's gone to a nursing home to rest and get better,
so Dad brought Chloe and me to see him. He's got crutches
and says his new hip is working better than the old one.
He has to do lots of exercises and walk a bit every day.

Granddad said that he had a dream about you just after
his operation.

He said that you were standing beside his bed and that
you smiled and told him not to worry, that he'd be fine.

He's going home next Wednesday which is good because
I think Granny really misses him.

Love,
Lucie x

Dear Mum,

It's Pancake Tuesday - Mardi Gras!

I knew that I'd find a recipe for crêpes or pancakes in your recipe book because you always loved making them.

Chloe and I mixed the pancake batter and Dad and Hugo got all the toppings ready. We had hot chocolate sauce, ice cream, maple syrup, lemon and caster sugar.

We put on two small frying pans and everyone took a turn trying to make one. Dad and Chloe really showed off flipping their ones. Dad's nearly fell on the floor, but he caught it in the nick of time.

The pancakes were scrummy and it's so long since we made pancakes. We haven't had any since you got sick.

'Your mum was the queen of pancakes, but tonight we proved that we can learn how to cook them too,' Dad said.

I'm so glad we have your recipe book.

Love,

Lucie x

P.S. Mémé phoned and she was making pancakes too.

Pancakes/Crêpes

Ingredients
3 eggs
150 grams plain flour
400ml of milk
Butter or oil for frying

Method
Mix the eggs and flour and milk together in a bowl. Melt a knob of butter in a frying pan and when it is hot put two spoonfuls or a small ladle of pancake batter into the frying pan.

Watch carefully as it begins to cook on one side and when it is done turn it over. Serve quickly while still warm!

Dear Mum,

Today I have a question. What do you do if you see something or someone you know do something they shouldn't be doing? Do you tell or do you keep it secret?

I asked Dad and he said that people often 'shoot the messenger', which I think means people blame the person who gives them bad news. I am not a telltale tattler, but I just don't know what to do. . .

On Saturday I saw Tim with a girl with dark hair and big earrings, who was wearing a denim skirt and boots. Tim was holding her hand, and while we were stopped at the lights he kissed her. She is *definitely* not his sister or friend. I was in Amy's mum's car so he didn't see me. Well, I don't think he did.

Amy says I should tell, especially since it is about my sister, and Jess says I definitely shouldn't. Remember when Auntie Maria found out about Uncle Chris cheating on her. Even though they are divorced, she still never speaks to the friend who told her. I don't want Chloe to be mad at me.

Mum, it's an awful secret and when I see Chloe phoning

and texting Tim and going around humming their favourite song I feel sick. What will happen when she finds out?!

Tim is coming over on Saturday night and he and Chloe are babysitting Hugo and me, as Dad is going out for dinner with some friends. I will stay in my room. I don't want to even see him. Hugo likes Tim, but I am going to ignore him. He can't treat my big sister like that!

What should I do?

Love,
Lucie x

Dear Mum,

When I got home from school Chloe was upstairs in bed.

She came home early from school and Auntie Trish had to collect her.

'Chloe's not feeling too well so don't you go disturbing her.'

Chloe never gets sick so I was worried about her. I was changing in my bedroom when I heard her crying: big heavy awful sad tears.

'Are you OK Chloe?' I asked, knocking on her door.

'Go away,' she roared. 'Don't come in! Leave me alone!'

'Are you sick?'

'Leave me alone!'

I did leave her alone and went downstairs and did my homework and helped Hugo with his.

Auntie Trish made lemon chicken and rice because she knows it's Chloe's favourite food.

'I'm not hungry!' she roared down. 'I'm not eating.'

Dad had to go to a big work conference and there is a

dinner afterwards so he won't be home until later, so Auntie Trish stayed with us and went up to the bedroom to talk to Chloe.

Chloe was crying, and must be feeling really awful because she didn't eat any dinner or come downstairs even once.

Mum, please don't let her be sick and have to go to the hospital.

Love,
Lucie x

Saturday 25th February

Dear Mum,

Chloe still won't get out of bed. She wouldn't go to school yesterday. Maybe Dad should take her to the doctor.

'I don't think a doctor can cure what is wrong with your sister,' said Dad.

Poor Chloe looks awful. Her face is all puffy and her eyes are red and she is all rolled up in her duvet and won't even listen to music.

'Get out!' she yells if any of us go near her.

I went over to Amy's for a while this afternoon and we went for a cycle to the park and the shops. When I got back Dad was making the dinner.

'Go tell your sister she is to get up. Trish has left some of that chicken thing she likes for her to eat.'

'I'm not hungry,' she shouted at me 'and I'm staying in bed.'

Dad got angry when he heard that she wouldn't come down for dinner. He said that we've had enough of people being really sick in this house and if Chloe didn't come down for tea in ten minutes he was coming up to get her. Chloe knew Dad meant it and came down in her pyjamas for dinner.

She wouldn't talk to us, but she must have been feeling a bit better as she ate some of the lemon chicken.

'Just to let you all know,' she said, 'Tim and I have broken up. He's not my boyfriend any more and that's the end of it. I don't even want to hear his name.'

I looked at the gravy on my plate. Mum, I promise I never said a word. I kept the secret.

'What happened?' asked Dad.

Chloe looked like she was going to cry. 'Tim is a two-timing creep,' she said. 'I was walking through the playground on Thursday and I saw him with another girl. They were waiting for the bus and holding hands. She's in his year in school and they used to go out before and now are going out again . . . something Tim *forgot* to tell me. I tried to phone and text him, but he wouldn't answer me.'

I didn't know what to say. I told Chloe I was sorry.

'He broke my heart and smashed it to pieces,' she said, and I felt awful for her.

'At least now you won't be Mrs Frosty,' said Hugo.

We burst out laughing; even Chloe giggled.

'Heartbreak hurts,' that's what Chloe said later when we
were talking. 'You love someone, you lose them!'

I don't think I ever, ever want to fall in love and get my
heart broken like Chloe. My heart is already sore and
broken enough because I lost you!

'I really wish Mum was here,' said Chloe.

I wish you were here too.

Love,

Lucie x

Mum,

Dad came into my room tonight when I was in the middle of writing to you.

'It's late, Lucie, you should be asleep. What are you doing?' he asked

'I'm just writing a letter.'

'Who are you writing to?'

I was going to lie and say 'Mémé', but then I told him that it was to you and that I wrote to you all the time. Dad didn't know what to say at first.

'You write to Mum?'

'Yes. I like writing to her.'

'Your mum was always writing letters too you know. When we first met and she went back to France she wrote to me for months. I still have all the letters, saying how she felt, telling me what she was doing. It meant that even though we were far apart we still felt so close. When we got married there were always little letters and notes from her; she scribbled everywhere. Lucie, you are so like her with your letters and words . . . . able to express yourself in a way that I wish I could.'

Dad looked at me for a few minutes and then he went off back to his room.

Mum, I miss you so much sometimes it hurts, like a really bad pain.

Love,
Lucie x

Spring

Mum,

Our garden is covered with daffodils! They are everywhere, in the flower beds, up the driveway and under the lilac tree. All the bulbs that you planted have opened. Seeing yellow daffodils all over the garden makes me think of you. You always said that daffodils were your favourite flower, not just because they are so pretty and colourful, but because they make you smile and forget the cold bad grey wet days of winter and seem to say *spring is here, the sun is shining, be happy, be cheerful.*

I am *trying* Mum! It's hard, but I really am trying and your daffodils are helping.

Thanks for planting them.

Love,
Lucie x

Dear Mum,

Some days when I wake up in the morning I close my eyes and pretend that you are downstairs in the kitchen making breakfast and getting our school lunches ready, loading the dishwasher, singing – you always sing in the morning.

Then I get up and go downstairs and make my own breakfast and school lunch. . .

I really miss hearing you sing.

Love,
Lucie x

Saturday 3rd March

Mum,

Dad sold your car today. None of us wanted him to sell
it, but he said that if nobody drives the car the engine
will stop working.

It's been sitting out in the driveway since you got too
sick to drive and Dad has recharged the battery four
times already.

Chloe had an argument with him about it because she
wanted him to keep your car until she was eighteen and
able to drive it, but Dad said no way. Your car is far too
big for someone only learning how to drive.

We are all upset about it as we love your car. Hugo
wanted us to keep the car forever, but he knows we can't
do that.

I remember when you bought the car, you were so
happy! You decided to name it Daisy because you
wanted it to have a pretty name. Whenever I look at
it it makes me think of you driving us everywhere
because you loved it so much! You'd drive us to school,
to Granny's, to the shops, to birthday parties, to the

doctor's, to the park and the big adventure playground, to McDonald's, the swimming pool, the cinema and the zoo and to the beach during the summer. We loved going in that car and are really going to miss it because it is so much part of our family . . . part of you.

Dad said the garage wouldn't take it because it's old, so he washed and polished it, so it looked really good, and then he put it up for sale on the internet. A few people came to see it and Dad sold it to a couple who have two little boys and a baby girl and need a family-size car. It's nice that another family will be able to use Daisy, but none of us want someone else driving your car because it makes us feel like another part of you is gone.

Chloe says Dad was probably glad to sell the car and get the money, but I think he misses Daisy too. I really do.

Love (and hugs and kisses),
Lucie x

Dear Mum,

Tonight when I went into the study to get some paper I heard a *tap . . . tap . . . tapping* on the computer. I thought it was Dad or Chloe, but when I opened the door there was no one there, the computer wasn't even on, but I heard it, I really did!

It was you . . . I'm sure it was. . .

You used to love working on the computer when we were home from school or at night, *tap . . . tap . . . tapping* away quietly.

I miss that sound and miss you every day.

Love,

Lucie x

Mum,

If you are a ghost or spirit, what does that mean?

I looked it up on Dad's computer and got lots of different answers...

*The soul of a dead person, a disembodied spirit imagined, usually as a vague, shadowy or evanescent form, as wandering among or haunting living persons.

*An apparition of a dead person which is believed to appear or become manifest to the living, typically as a nebulous image.

*The spirit of a dead person, especially one believed to appear in bodily likeness to living persons or to haunt former habitats.

*A demon or spirit.

*A returning or haunting memory or image.

*The spirit of a dead person that someone sees or hears

Well I do see or hear you sometimes. You often appear to

me and you are a bit vague and shadowy. But you are not a demon and you don't haunt or scare me. . . When you do come to me or I sense you . . . I like it.

I saw a programme on TV about a lady who can talk to ghosts and they talk to her. I wish I could do that, then we could talk together like we used to. . .

I like seeing you or sensing you and knowing you are still around us and haven't left . . . yet.

Love,
Lucie x

Mum,
I'm writing to you again tonight because I have to tell you that:

I HATE CHLOE!

I just found her in my bedroom snooping around! She was reading my letters to you and going through my personal stuff.

She has no right to come in here and do that!

She said she only wanted to borrow my black ink pen, and that I was a weirdo with my letters and books and writing. . . How can she be my sister?

We're so different, we don't look one bit alike and we've absolutely nothing in common. All she cares about is clothes and boys and make-up!

I HATE her and I told her to get out and stay out of my room forever!

Love,
Lucie x

Mum,

Dad went to my parent-teacher meeting this afternoon. I was really worried about what Mrs Martin might say about me.

Yesterday we put up all our Arts and Craft stuff around the classroom for the parents to see. All our essays and stories and poems about the Titanic were on display too.

When Dad got home he said that Mrs Martin had been really nice about me and told Dad that I was a very good student . . . one of her best. Can you believe it, Mum? One of her best students! Dad said he was very proud of me and how I've managed in a very 'difficult' year. Dad met lots of other parents there, but he was the only dad on his own.

Love,
Lucie x

8th March

Mum,

Chloe and Hugo are sick. Chloe stayed home from school
yesterday because she had a temperature and felt awful.
She only had a bit of potato for dinner, but she got sick in
the blue bowl after she ate it. It was so yucky.

Hugo said he felt sick too, but Dad didn't believe him and
sent him to school today!

Then, after lunch, Hugo's teacher Mr Loftus came into my
classroom and said that Hugo needed me urgently. Mum,
it was awful! Hugo was sick in class . . . it was all over the
floor and his desk! It really smelled and Hugo was crying
so much, all he wanted was you. The school phoned Dad
and he picked us up.

When we got home Hugo changed into his pyjamas and
went straight to bed.

He looked so white and felt really hot, even though he
said he was freezing cold.

I think Dad's worried about taking some much time off
work; he keeps saying how hard it is to look after everyone

and do his job. He said it was a 'juggling act and someday
something is going to come crashing to the floor!'

Dad hates people being sick, especially anyone from our
family. I think it reminds him of how you were . . . It was
so disgusting for him having to wash Hugo's sicky school
uniform. Mum, please make Hugo stop puking!

Love,
Lucie x

Dear Mum,

Puke is the grossest thing EVER! Hugo puked all over his own bed and then puked in yours and Dad's. It was *disgusting* and Dad had to change both beds because Chloe said she was too sick to help and I nearly threw up myself as the smell was so bad.

Dad put everything in the washing machine and washed the carpet in your bedroom, but the house still smells terrible. Dad said that he's going to get extra strong air freshener in the supermarket and this morning he left some of the windows open.

I still had to go to school, but Lara came over early to look after Chloe and Hugo so that Dad could go to work. She made hot lemon and ginger and garlic drinks for everyone. She says that's what everyone takes in Moldova if they get a cold or flu. It is the most disgusting thing you have ever tasted or smelled.

Love,

Lucie x

Mum,

Hugo is really sick. He keeps saying: 'I want Mum. Where's Mummy?'

Poor Hugo, he just wants you.

Now Dad's got a bad cough and a temperature too, so Dr Nicholls had to come to the house. He said they all have the flu and gave them some medicine.

With three people sick in the house I'm like a nurse! I spent the whole day getting drinks and tissues for everyone, and trying to mind them.

Granny wanted to come over to help with the cooking and washing, but Dad says he doesn't want to risk her or Granddad getting it. He won't even let me go over to Amy's or any of my friends.

It's not fair being stuck at home with everyone coughing and so sick!

I wish you were here, Mum, as you know what to do when people are sick and how to get them better. It shouldn't be up to me to look after everyone else!

I can't wait for Monday so I can go to school and see all my friends!

Love,
(Nurse) Lucie x

Dear Mum,

Hugo tossed and turned all night in his sleep. When he woke up he said that you were there sitting beside his bed, watching him, and that your hands were cool and soft and you told him not to be afraid that he would be fine.

Dad said that he was dreaming, but I don't think it was a dream . . . I think Hugo really saw you. He needed you and you came . . . He asked me if you are a ghost.

I didn't want to scare him, but I told him you are . . . but a good one . . . a very good ghost.

Love (and hugs and kisses),
Lucie x

Dear Mum,

Now I'm sick too! Mrs Martin sent me home from school on Monday. Roz had to come and collect me as Dad's too sick to drive.

I feel awful and my throat and head really hurt. I went straight to bed and slept. It was dark when I woke up and I was so hot. Chloe brought me a glass of ice-cold 7Up and changed my bed while I was in the bathroom so I could lie down on cool fresh sheets and pillowcases just like you always used to do when we were sick.

She sat beside me till I felt sleepy again. 'I'm only next door if you need me,' she promised, 'and I'll leave the door open.'

Today my legs feel kind of wobbly and my throat is so sore. I just want to sleep all the time with the quilt up around me. I don't feel like reading or even watching the TV and when Lara hoovered the noise really hurt my head. I hate being sick and wish you were here to look after me.

Everyone is usually busy doing their own stuff . . . Chloe on Facebook or on the phone, Hugo playing his games, Dad working so hard and me stuck in my books and writing. But now we've all had to really try to care for each other, the way you used to . . . each one of us helping the other. It's kind of weird but I think that being sick has brought us together. . .

Chloe tried cooking dinner for us tonight. She made chicken and noodles but it made me feel sick.

Love,
Lucie x
P.S. Mum, I just wish you were here.

17th March

Mum,

This is the worst St Patrick's Day *ever!*

Everyone's having fun today except us. We watched a DVD and Dad ordered a Chinese takeaway. Chloe's all upset and angry because Dad wouldn't allow her to go to the big St Patrick's disco tonight with all her friends.

I couldn't even eat any of the take-away and just had a bowl of cereal instead.

Love,
Lucie x

Happy Mother's Day Mum!

I hope you like the card. I've put all the things you love on it: the garden, our robin, music and a shining sun.

Last year, even though you were sick, we went to the nice Italian restaurant down near the seafront in Dun Laoghaire for Mother's Day. We walked along the pier and got big ice-cream cones for dessert. I remember you got an extra scoop of chocolate chip because the next day you had to go into hospital for your chemotherapy and you knew that it would make you feel sick and tired and not able to eat.

Granny has gone to visit Maria in London so today we just stayed home, remembering you and what a wonderful mum you are . . . were. . . You are the best mum ever.

I hope that you and all the mums in heaven have a Happy Mother's Day!

All my love and hugs,
Lucie x

P.S. Mémé and Poppa are coming to see us in two weeks time.

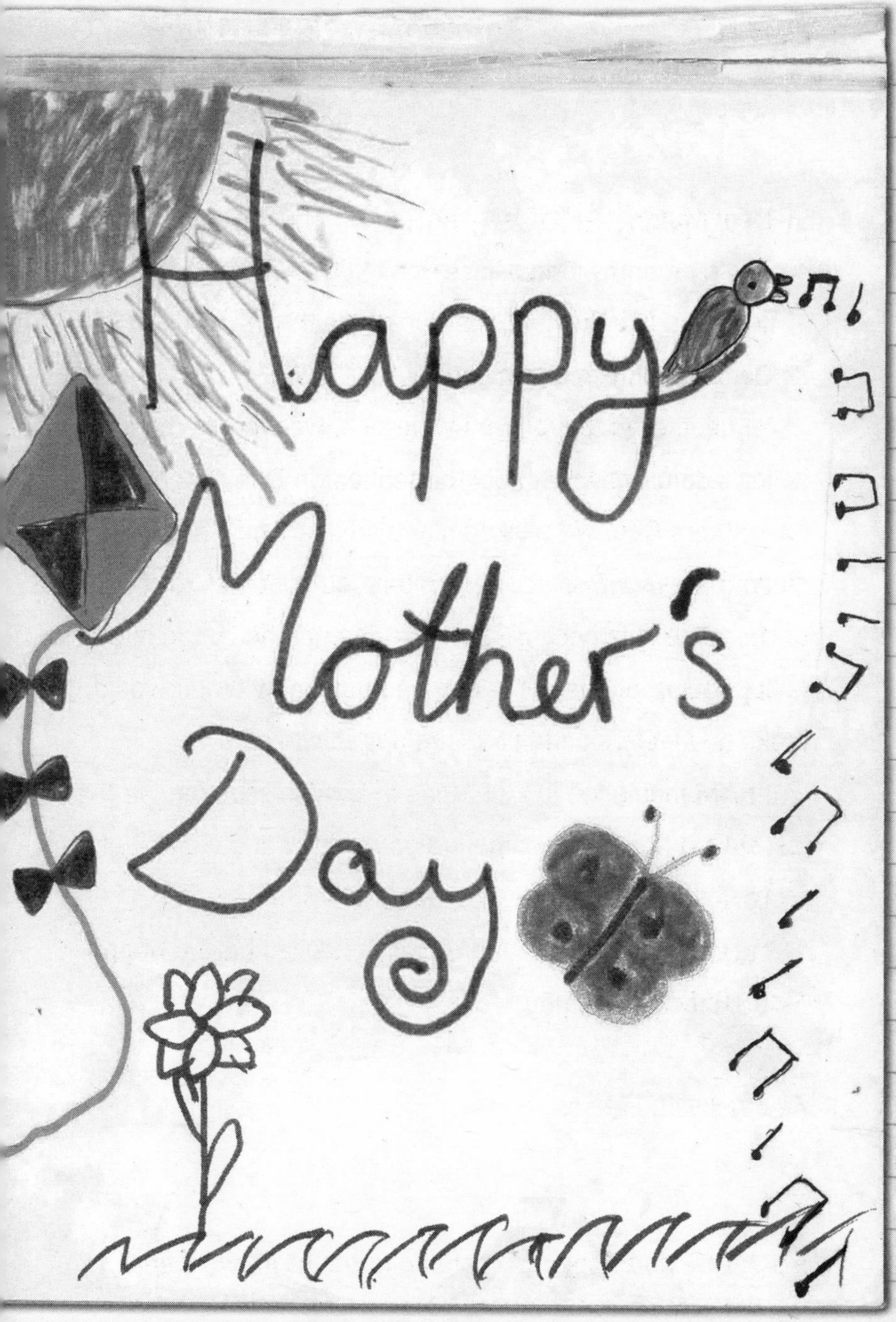
Happy
Mother's
Day

20th March

Dear Mum,

 Its six months today since you left us.

Over 180 days without you.

I still don't know why you had to die.

Why *my* mum?

It's not fair.

I HATE today.

Love,

Lucie x

P.S. I really miss you.

22nd March

Mum,

Chloe is in a seriously bad mood all the time! She's so skinny that you can see some of her bones and her school skirt is falling off her. When I said to her about being too skinny she said it was only because she'd been sick and to mind my own business!

Being sick made me think about you when you were sick. You were ill for such a long time and had to stay in bed most of the time. I remember how tired you were; sometimes the cancer made you too tired to even talk. One of us would read you a bit from a paper or a magazine or a book and sit with you. I used to read you 'Winnie the Pooh' because it made you smile.

Are there books in heaven?

I wish that I could still read to you.

Love,
Lucie x

Dear Mum,

Auntie Trish is going to have a baby!

We went to Auntie Trish and Uncle Alan's for dinner and when we were all sitting down they told us. Auntie Trish said that it was a miracle because they have been trying for a baby for such a long time. She was so excited and she said: 'Madeleine definitely had something to do with this!'

Did you, Mum?

Granny was crying and Dad and Granddad didn't know what to say and everyone was really excited for them. Uncle Alan opened a bottle of champagne and we all got to have a taste – even Hugo! It was very fancy and they had set the dining table with their good glasses, and candles, flowers and everything.

Auntie Trish is so happy. She's gone mad eating wine gums and tortilla chips, but not together!

The baby is due in September. I can't wait. Auntie Trish

says that she is going to need lots of helpers when it
arrives.

I'm so excited that we are getting a new cousin.

Love,
Lucie x

Dear Mum,

Hugo and I went to Anna's for our session this evening but Chloe wouldn't come. She says she doesn't need to talk to Anna any more, but Dad says she still does.

He keeps asking me about Chloe's eating.

We all know Chloe doesn't eat much. Sometimes she just pretends to eat! She always comes to the table after everyone else and finishes first, clearing her plate and putting it in the dishwasher even if we are still eating dinner.

Chloe's always talking to her friends about boys and how they only like thin girls. I think Chloe's super skinny, but she's so mad she still thinks her tummy and bum are big! Now she's gone crazy and started running after school. She wants to join a gym, but Dad says it's too expensive. She says Dad is useless and doesn't understand about girls needing to be thin.

Dad said I wasn't to say anything to Chloe or make a big deal about it, but that if I notice her behaving oddly or if she talks to me about it I should tell him. I just wish she would come to Anna's with us. Anna's a really good listener. She says that it's the most important part of her job.

Hugo talked to Anna about his bad dreams. He also told her that he got in a fight at school with two big boys who were teasing him about the fact that his trousers had a hole in them. They asked why his mum didn't fix them or buy him a new pair and he pushed one of them really hard and told him to leave him alone. He said they won't come near him again. . .

Anna asked how things were going since my last visit and I told her about seeing you sometimes. She said that maybe I miss you so much that I want to try and hold on to you and not let you go.

Maybe that's what Hugo's doing too with his dreams? I know that Dad dreams about you too sometimes. I hear him call out your name in the middle of the night and then he gets up and goes down to the kitchen on his own and makes coffee or turns on the computer.

Anna says it takes time . . . time . . . time . . . but that one day it won't hurt so much to know that you're gone. I don't think that it will ever stop hurting.

Love,
Lucie x

Saturday 31st March

Mum,

It's Dad's birthday so Chloe and I made him a special big birthday breakfast with bacon and sausages and pudding and beans and toast. He said he was in no mood to celebrate being a year older, but we wanted him to have a proper birthday. We gave him a new dock for his iPod and a book of guitar songs that he's wanted for ages and a big jar of jelly beans.

Later on Granny and Granddad and Auntie Trish and Uncle Alan came over for dinner to celebrate with us.

Granny and Granddad got Dad a fancy new SatNav for the car, and Auntie Trish got him a CD and a bottle of wine.

Chloe, Hugo and I cooked a proper dinner for everyone. We made French pâté and toast for a starter, then lasagne and salad, and finally a big chocolate birthday cake for dessert. It's the one you used to always make for all our birthdays, and it's Dad's favourite cake. We put candles on it and all sang 'Happy Birthday' to Dad. The cake tasted amazing! But it still wasn't as good as yours used to be. . .

After dinner Auntie Trish made Dad get out the guitar and try out some songs from the new book. I played two songs and Granddad sang along with us too.

Hugo fell asleep on the couch and Dad lifted him up to bed. At least we have no school tomorrow and can all sleep in.

Bonne nuit!

Love,

Lucie x

P.S. I wish you were here singing with us.

Bon Anniversaire
Gâteau au Chocolat

Ingredients

150 grams caster sugar
150 grams self-raising flour
150 grams margarine
3 large eggs
50 grams drinking chocolate
6 tablespoons hot water
2 teaspoons baking powder
A pinch of salt
150 grams-200 grams icing sugar, sifted

Method

· Preheat oven to 190C. Grease two cake tins.

· Dissolve drinking chocolate in hot water.

· Beat eggs. Then mix in the chocolate and all the rest of the ingredients until the mixture is smooth.

· Divide the mixture between the two tins and place in the oven for around 25 minutes. Then turn out on to a wire rack to cool.

· Mix the sifted icing sugar with water and stir with a spoon till the icing is thin enough to spread on the cake but not too runny.

Spread the icing on the top of one cake then put the other cake on top of it and use the rest of the icing to cover it.

Mum,

Hurray! We start our Easter holidays today. Chloe and
I did the shopping in Tesco tonight while Dad and Hugo
went off to get their hair cut. Chloe is so annoying, as she
disappeared off to look at the magazine and DVD section
and left me with the shopping list.

The supermarket was really busy! While I was waiting for
Chloe near the checkout queue I saw a lady who looked
so white and tired and thin that she reminded me of you
when you were very sick.

She had a scarf on her head like you used to wear when
you were having chemo and she had no eyelashes or
eyebrows either. Her trolley looked too heavy for her to
push and I remembered how hard it was for you when you
had to go shopping.

I knew Chloe would be ages so I asked if she wanted
any help.

'that's very kind. Are you sure you don't mind!' she said,
showing me her list.

'Yes, my mum was sick last year and I used to help her.'

It only took a few minutes, but we soon got everything she needed and I wheeled her trolley to the checkout and lifted her groceries on to the belt.

'thank you so much. Your mother must be so proud to have such a good daughter. How is she now? How is she doing?'

I didn't know what to say . . . I couldn't tell her so I lied.

'She's fine. She's better again . . . much better.'

'that's good to hear. Thank you again.'

Mum, was it bad to lie to her? I just had to.

Dad and Hugo picked us up from the supermarket. They both had their hair cut really short. It makes Hugo look older, especially now that he's grown quite a bit taller too. He looks more grown-up every day.

All I keep thinking about is the lady in the supermarket. I wonder if she has a family and kids . . . I hope she gets better.

Love,
Lucie x

Mum,

This morning when Hugo and I were cycling in the park I saw you.

You were sitting on a bench down near the duck pond in your warm red jacket. You smiled over at us.

You looked so beautiful and happy, and your hair had all grown back and was long again. Hugo ran off to the playground to go on the slide and I could see you watching him. I ran over towards you, but when I got near you just disappeared.

I waited ages and ages to see if you would come back, but you didn't. Then it started to rain and we sheltered under the trees with our bikes. When it stopped raining I looked and looked for you, but you were gone.

Love,

Lucie x

P.S. It was you, wasn't it?

P.P.S. Mémé and Poppa are coming tomorrow!!

Happy Easter, Mum!

We got lots of Easter eggs. Dad got us some and Mémé and Poppa brought some from France too! The house is full of chocolate.

Yesterday we all went to dinner in Max's Bistro. Poppa had snails . . . *yeuk!*

Dad did an Easter Egg Hunt for us in the garden this morning, but he made it so hard that Hugo and I couldn't find some of them, so he had to give us a few clues!

We all went to Easter Sunday mass together and then we went to the graveyard and put some lovely flowers on your grave. Mémé got really sad and upset and we said some prayers. The graveyard looks different to the last time we visited, now there are bluebells and daffodils growing everywhere. I think you'd really like it.

We got another Easter egg each when we all went to Granny's for lunch. Mémé says that Granny has a heart as big as a house and that she is so glad that we live close to her and Granddad.

Granny did a big roast and put bowls of little pink and yellow eggs on the table with little fluffy Easter chicks.

You used to put little chicks and rabbits and lambs on the table at Easter and we would all paint some real eggs and hang them with ribbon from branches of catkins in the big glass vase in the hall and kitchen. Remember the Easter Bunny play that Chloe, Hugo and I would put on with our hand puppets?

I loved those silly plays and stories about our three bunnies doing all sorts of crazy things trying to hide eggs and find eggs and then eating far too many eggs.

We didn't paint any eggs this year and we didn't do our play. It wouldn't have been the same without you.

Love (and bunny hugs),

Lucie x

10th April

Mum,

It was really sunny today so we went to visit Powerscourt Gardens yesterday with Mémé and Poppa. We walked all around and had afternoon tea in the restaurant.

The Japanese garden is full of cherry blossom. I wish they could stay longer, but Poppa said that they have to go back to Paris tomorrow morning.

So we won't see them again until the summer holidays.

The red tulips I helped you to plant last year are all opening up. They are like a big red surprise from you and are so cool. Mémé took some photos of them with her camera because they look so beautiful.

Jess came over today. She's upset because her mum and dad told her over Easter that they are going to get a divorce. I think she hoped that they would stop fighting and get back together and be a family again, but now everything is going to be shared and split down the middle, and that includes Jess. Poor Jess.

Tomorrow we are going to Megan's birthday party. She's having a sleepover and a lot of the girls in our class are invited. Maybe it will help to cheer Jess up. Granny got me new pyjamas and I'm going to take Chloe's pink sleeping bag.

Love,
Lucie x

Dear Mum,

When I went to Megan's sleepover party I saw her new baby brother Finn; he's so cute and looks just like Megan. Her mum made us fajitas with lots of fillings and there was a big birthday cake and then we watched a DVD.

Afterwards we all got into our pyjamas and spread our sleeping bags on the floor in the living room.

Megan said we were going to tell ghost stories and she turned off the lights. We lit a few candles and Natalie said if we all sat in a circle and held hands and concentrated we could try to have a seance and contact a ghost or a spirit.

I didn't want to have the seance, but everyone else did, even Amy.

It was awful. The room was so quiet and Natalie blew out the candles so it was really dark too.

We were all sitting there when Natalie said she could feel someone, the ghost of a woman. Everyone looked at me, but I knew it wasn't you, because if you're around I can sense you. Then Natalie said it was a very old woman.

Megan said it might be her granny, who died two years ago. She said to ask if her granny was OK.

I could feel Amy squeezing my hand really tight. We were both soooo frightened.

'She said to tell you that she and Jackie are OK,' Natalie said.

'Who's Jackie?' asked Megan. 'My granddad was called Bill.'

'I think that's my granny,' whispered Amy. 'She had a little dog called Jackie. They were always together. It must be my granny.'

The message was for Amy!

Then Natalie said there was a boy in the room. He was standing behind us. All we could hear was the sound of our breathing, and the beat of our hearts.

Jess said she could sense the boy too. He was in a uniform. I was so scared I was almost shaking. Everybody kept saying things about him as if they could see him too: he had dark hair. He had green eyes. His leg was bleeding.

Jess thought he was a soldier.

Ruth said he could be her cousin Dylan, an American soldier who was killed in Afghanistan two years ago. He

was only nineteen and was blown up by a landmine.
She'd never met him.

It was awful and really scary.

If it was Dylan he didn't give any message.

Suddenly Megan's mum came in and put on the lights.
She'd made popcorn for us and said we could have one
more DVD before we went to sleep.

Sometimes Natalie is so annoying. I bet she's seen the
photo of Amy's Granny and her dog Jackie in their living
room. We all have . . . But none of us knew about Ruth's
cousin.

On our way home the next morning Amy kept on at me
about why I didn't try and contact you during the seance.
Didn't I want to try to talk to you or see you again? Didn't
I want to speak to you, see your spirit? Didn't I believe in
the next world, the afterlife?

Mum, I didn't know what to say. I couldn't tell Amy that
I still see you and feel you around me all the time and
that I don't need a seance or candles to sense that you're
close by. I told her that I think seances are stupid and that
people who believe in them are stupid too. Then she got

cross with me and stormed off.

I'm so annoyed with her. All she kept going on about was her granny and her dog Jackie and how she couldn't wait to tell her mum all about them when she got home.

I'm so tired that I'm finishing this letter and going to bed early.

Love,
Lucie x

13th April

Mum,

I'm NOT talking to Amy.

Sometimes she is *so* stupid.

Chloe says that I'm being stupid and that we should make it up, but I don't want to!

Love,
Lucie x

Sunday 15th April

Mum,

Something incredible has happened . . . WE GOT A DOG!
His name is Buddy and we got him yesterday.

Dad told us that we all had to get up early and go somewhere with him. Chloe, as usual, said that she didn't want to come. But Dad said everyone had to come as it was an 'important family outing'. We drove to a place outside Dublin where there were lots of farms and fields. Dad wouldn't tell us where we were going until he stopped the car at the Kildare Animal Centre and we could hear lots of dogs barking from out on the road. We all looked at him like he was mad, and he said that he'd been thinking about it and that maybe Hugo was right, our family needs a dog.

We couldn't believe it. Dad changed his mind! Hugo was so excited. He's wanted a dog for so long and now we were going to get one.

Mrs O'Malley, who runs the rescue centre, showed us the big barn with all the new puppies. They were so tiny and cute. Some were with their mothers and others were in baskets and blankets, and there were lamps to keep them warm. Chloe wanted us to get a brand-new puppy that was only a few weeks old, but Dad said they are too small and too much work. Mrs O'Malley said they take a while to settle in and often miss their mothers and brothers and sisters.

Then we went to the big yard which has wire all around and there were about twenty dogs there. They weren't new puppies, but were still young dogs. Big ones, little ones, tiny ones, all sorts of dogs with sad eyes and waggly tails, barking, all excited, wanting someone to take them home.

It was so sad because nobody wanted them and Hugo and I wanted to rescue them all, but Dad said . . . ONE DOG ONLY!

It was so hard to pick. We all wanted different ones: I saw a cute little white Westie, Dad liked a big golden retriever and Chloe spotted a yappy little Yorkshire. Hugo didn't say anything and just walked around all the dogs, looking. One dog kept following him. He had shaggy white hair and a brown patch on his ear and one around his eye and the longest hairy tail you ever saw. He was really skinny-looking and Mrs O'Malley said he was a stray someone found on the beach that had been neglected and was starving, but that he was a really good dog and very friendly.

The dog licked Dad's hand. He snuffled his nose against me and let Chloe scratch behind his ears. Hugo really wanted to get him.

'Is everyone sure? You all realise that everyone in the house will have to help look after him and walk him and care for him . . . a dog is a big responsibility.'

We all nodded. He was the dog we wanted.

The dog sat on Hugo's lap on the way home in the car and peed on him! When we got home the dog ran around all over the house barking and then went out and dug a hole in the garden, and then came in and sat under the kitchen table while we were eating lunch.

In the afternoon we went and got him a bed, a lead, three dog bowls, a brush, some dog food and lots of doggy toys.

It feels different having a dog in the house. Kind of like another person has moved in.

We didn't know what to call him and tested out lots of names. Then Hugo said Buddy and we all liked it.

In the middle of the night Buddy began to howl and bark and woke us up.

Dad went downstairs to try to get him to stop before he woke the neighbours. Buddy ran up the stairs and straight into Hugo's room and curled up on his floor mat and wouldn't budge. Dad says dogs should not be let upstairs . . . but Buddy slept there last night. Hugo says that he is guarding him.

Mum, I wish that you could see Buddy. I know that you would love him too.

Wuff, wuff, wuff!

Love,
Lucie (and Buddy) x

Mum,

Buddy is great! He cocks his ear when you call his name and always wants to play.

He sleeps in with Hugo. Dad says it's OK because Hugo hasn't had a bad dream in the past few days, so maybe Buddy is helping him feel safe. We all feel safer in the house with Buddy. It's as if we have a guard dog, though he mostly just barks at cats and birds.

Dad took him for a walk tonight. And Chloe and I take turns brushing him.

When Lara came yesterday she complained that the house was full of dog hair. I don't think she likes dogs and thinks Buddy is messy and smelly. But we all love him.

Love,
Lucie x

Mum,

Today was one of the days I missed you most.
It wasn't because anything special happened, but
sometimes even small things make me sad because I
can't talk to you about them. Now I realise how much I
took for granted being able to talk to you about school
and friends and . . . anything!

When you died I wanted to die too because I didn't
think I could live without you. It's been seven months
and sometimes when I think of it I feel a pain that hurts
so much I can hardly breathe. It's like something sharp
stuck into me. On the outside I might look okay but
inside I feel awful.

Anna says it is grief and grief causes pain.

She said that I'll have bad days and sad days, but that
is OK because in time, some days will be better than
others and happy days will come.

Chloe came to see Anna again with us this week. She
knows she needs to go because she gets so upset about

what happened to you. Maybe that's why she won't eat!

Love (and kisses and hugs),

Lucie x

Mum

Dad took us to see the big Tutankhamun Exhibition at Simmonscourt today. Chloe wouldn't come as she said it was boring and she wanted to go shopping with some of her friends. I think they were meeting some boys as she wore her best jeans and new blue top. Dad was really annoyed with her but I'm glad that she didn't come with us.

The exhibition was of replicas of all the treasures that an explorer called Howard Carter discovered when he found the tomb of Tutankhamun in Egypt and opened it.

Tutankhamun became the king of Egypt when he was a boy and his people worshipped him. When he died he was buried inside a hidden tomb with all his gold and riches and even his chariot and hunting bows. He was in a big sarcophagus which was hidden inside two other ones and he was wrapped up like a mummy with a gold mask on his head.

Hugo and I thought it was like in the film 'The Mummy' or 'Raiders of the Lost Ark'. Being an archaeologist must be such a cool job, going on digs and finding treasures and artefacts.

The Egyptians really believed in an afterlife and thought you had to bring everything you owned to the next life by burying it with you. So Tutankhamun had loads of stuff with him!

Mum, what is the afterlife really like? Is it scary there or happy? And do you miss people like we miss you?

Love,
Lucie x

25th April

Mum,

Chloe told me she hates her life, her braces, the way she looks and most of all being nearly sixteen.

It's going to be her birthday soon, but she doesn't want to be grown up, be the strong one and do adult stuff for everyone. She's fed up of doing it now when she's fifteen, and she thinks that when she turns sixteen it will be a hundred times worse.

We had a big talk about everything. It feels like forever since Chloe told me anything! We talked about you too, Mum. Chloe said that with her birthday coming up all she can think about is how different things are without you. How you won't be here when she finishes school, starts college or gets her first job, or when she gets married, or has kids . . . I guess I'd never really thought about all that kind of stuff, the stuff we will be missing. It makes me really sad too thinking about you not being here for when I'm older.

Chloe said she wished you had told us the truth about

how sick you were, so that we would have known you weren't going to get better.

She said: 'Why didn't Mum tell us what we should do without her! I just want to talk to her and ask her what I'm supposed to do!'

I told her she could still talk to you . . . tell you how she feels . . . maybe she wouldn't feel so bad then. But Chloe just got really cross with me and told me that I was stupid to write these letters and pretend that you could read them. She said that you were dead and we all just have to get used to it. Then she stormed out of my room. . .

I didn't know what to say.

Mum, Chloe is so angry and upset. You told us to stick together to help each other and talk to each other. I wish Chloe would remember that. I'll just have to try harder.

Love,
Lucie x
P.S. Am I a snitch if I say something to Dad about Chloe?

Friday 27th April

Mum,

I told Dad.

I love Chloe and don't want her to be so sad and angry and lonely.

Chloe was mad at me, but she and Dad talked and talked for hours last night. Hugo and I stayed upstairs and played his Spiderman game.

We could hear Chloe crying and crying.

Chloe wouldn't talk to me this morning but Dad said everything was going to be OK.

Love,
Lucie x

Dear Mum,

Chloe is speaking to me again.

She met with Anna on her own, and Anna arranged
for her to see a lady called Wendy who helps teenagers,
especially those with food issues.

Dad and Chloe are getting on better too.

We all miss you so much,

Love,

Lucie x

Dear Mum,

Hugo, Buddy and I went to Granny and Granddad's for the weekend because Dad's gone to a football match in Manchester, with Uncle Alan and some friends. Chloe went to stay at Sinead's.

Granny showed me how to make proper puff pastry and we made an apple tart. She's going to give me a few cookery lessons. Someone in our house needs to be able to cook as Dad is useless and Chloe doesn't like cooking.

Auntie Trish came over for dinner too. We had roast chicken with the apple tart and ice cream for dessert. Auntie Trish says now she is eating for two she is really enjoying it. She showed us an ultrasound picture of the baby. Hugo and I were trying to see the baby's face and nose and eyes, and we could see the baby was sucking its thumb.

On Saturday we went to Enniskerry for a walk in the woods. Granddad has to use a stick after his operation. Buddy spotted a red squirrel and nearly went crazy. He was barking and trying to jump up a tree after it. He thinks that he can climb trees! Granddad took a great photo of the red squirrel on his phone; he said that red squirrels are endangered and protected as the grey squirrels are taking over the woods and countryside.

When we got home we were starving. Hugo and I helped Granny make Chicken Paprika. It's so simple that I wrote the recipe down so I could add it to your recipe book when I got home. I like the idea that I can keep cooking just like you and add my own favourite recipes to your book.

On Sunday after church we went to the park and then Granny and Granddad read the Sunday papers. Dad came over to collect us and have lunch with all of us. He said he had a great time watching Liverpool beat Manchester United. Granny said he needed a break away from us all.

Love,
Lucie x
P.S. Hugo really likes cooking too.

Chicken Paprika

Ingredients
4 chicken breasts
1 large onion (chopped)
1 large sweet red pepper
(chopped into strips)
2 tablespoons olive oil
1/2 tablespoon sugar
1 large tablespoon paprika
2 teaspoons plain flour or cornflour
500ml chickenstock

Method
· Heat the olive oil in a large
frying pan and fry the chopped
onions until they're almost golden
· Add in the chopped up chicken
breasts, stir and once the chicken
starts to cook begin to add in stock.
· Keep stirring and add the chopped red pepper,
paprika and the rest of the stock.
· Let cook and simmer
(so there are small bubbles NOT big ones!)
then add the sugar and stir.
· Mix the cornflour/flour with a little
bit of water in a cup and carefully
add to the chicken mixture to help
thicken it. Serve with rice or potatoes.
For special occasions add some cream to
the mixture just before serving.

8th May

Mum,

When I went to the bookshop to buy a birthday card for Chloe, Mr Humphrey came over to talk to me. He asked how everyone was doing and said how much he still misses you. It's nice to know that everyone still thinks about you.

He gave me two new children's books and asked if I would read them and then write him a review to let other kids know what I thought! Can you believe he thinks that people will listen to what I think?

Love,
Lucie (your little bookworm) x

Dear Mum,

Chloe is sweet sixteen today!

Dad gave her your present, the beautiful heart on a silver chain.

Chloe cried and cried, she really loves it and put it on straight away.

She said, 'this means that Mum was thinking of me . . . and even though she knew that she wouldn't be here for my birthday she bought it for me because she still wanted me to know she was thinking of me. It's like a message from her. . . '

Chloe keeps touching it. It's the best present ever as it's like a sign from you that you are close to her.

Dad got her a new iPod too; she couldn't believe it and spent ages uploading all her favourite songs on to it.

I got her a wrap to wear over her bikini and some lipgloss, and Hugo got her a T-shirt that she wanted. Mémé and Poppa sent her a bottle of her favourite perfume and mascara, and Gran is taking her into town next week to get new jeans and a jacket and a pair of shoes.

Chloe's so lucky that her birthday was on a Saturday as she could have her party on the actual day.

Dad organised for everyone to go paintballing! We all got guns and paint pellets and had to wear goggles and a special suit to protect our clothes. We all ran around a huge field trying to shoot each other with paint. It was seriously mad racing around splattering people and trying not to get splattered!

Chloe and her friends went to Little Italy afterwards. I know Chloe didn't want to have a birthday party, but I'm glad she did and I think she had fun.

Dad said that it's not every day you have a beautiful daughter turn sixteen.

I wish you were there with us, we all do. We miss you every single day, but things like birthdays and parties and holidays make it worse!

I love you so much,
Lucie x

Dear Mum,

Today at my guitar lesson Mr Handford said I had a 'real talent'.

I'm learning to play a new song which is really hard with lots of chords, but I love it. When I'm playing I forget about everything.

Mr Handford said I should think about auditioning for the school concert next autumn, but I think I'd be too scared to stand up in the school hall in front of everyone and play. I'd forget everything and get mixed up and do everything wrong.

Mr Handford said if I practise hard I'll get over my nerves but I have to practise . . . a lot.

What do you think I should do?

Did you ever get nervous when you played in front of people?

Love,

Lucie x

18th May

Mum,

Hugo's football team played in the school's semi-final today against St John's.

We all went to the match to support him. Granddad came too, and Conor is on the team so Roz and Johnny were there.

Hugo was really nervous, but he shouldn't have been! He's got really good at football this year and is really fast. He's got taller and isn't afraid to tackle and chase after the ball. When he scored a goal we all went crazy.

In the second half Hugo was so fast chasing the ball with Mark and Conor. He nearly scored another goal, but the ball went out. Sometimes Hugo seems so grown-up and not just my little brother.

St John's won so Hugo and his team were upset, but their teacher said that they all 'played their hearts out' and deserved to be back again next year trying to win THE CUP!

You would have been so proud of Hugo today.

Love,
Lucie x

Mum,

I saw you again last night. You were so still like a pale white statue standing at the bedroom window. You looked so sad.

What's it like being a ghost?

Is it lonely or scary?

It must feel weird.

It's been 240 days . . . eight months.

Still missing you.

Love,
Lucie x

Friday 25th May

Dear Mum,

It was Amy's birthday today and eight of us went to the cinema after school.

We went to see 'The Party Princess' which is about a girl in high school who wants to be rich and posh like a princess, and a princess who is bored with living in a castle and wants to go to school and be ordinary, and so they swap lives. It was brill! We went to Eddie Rocket's afterwards.

I got Amy a new charm for her bracelet and a bottle of purple nail varnish. She's big into purple at the moment. Her mum and dad got her a kitten! It's black with two white paws and is called Pixie. She showed us a photo on her phone.

I'm going over to Amy's tomorrow to see her.

Love,
Lucie x

Mum,

Dad went for drinks with some people from work tonight, so Chloe had to babysit me. Hugo went to stay at Conor's.

Chloe's friend Alex called over. He's really nice . . . much nicer than Tim, but she says he's 'just a friend' . . . nothing more. I like him, he's really funny. We all played on the Xbox for a while, but then they wanted to watch a DVD that Chloe said I was too young for . . . *boo, boo, boo!*

So Buddy and I went outside and sat in the back garden for ages.

Buddy's a funny dog and he likes looking at the stars too. Looking up at the night sky reminds me of you teaching me all about the stars and the constellations. The North Star, the Great Bear, the Little Bear. You always used to say that looking at the stars makes us seem small and makes us realise just how beautiful and big the universe is.

As I looked up I couldn't see you, but I know you were somewhere there in the darkness beside me.

Every time I look at the stars I think of you.

Love,
Lucie x

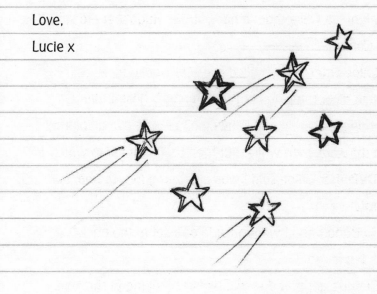

Summer

Dear Mum,

We had our school trip to Clara Lara, the big adventure park in Wicklow, today. It was brilliant. We sang on the bus the whole way there and back.

It rained yesterday so the ground was really wet and muddy, but we brought our boots and a change of clothes. The park is in the middle of a forest and is full of huge climbing frames and footbridges and rope bridges and is like a big obstacle course. Amy kept falling and got so covered in mud she looked like a mud-baby.

We were in teams and we did a big treasure hunt. We had maps and it took hours trying to find all the clues. We came second. It was great fun.

We had lunch in the picnic area and afterwards we went canoeing on the lake. The lake is HUGE and even though it was *freezing* we went for a swim. It was such fun with everybody running and jumping in and splashing each other.

It was the best school trip ever and we all want to go back next year!

I'm so tired tonight, I nearly fell asleep eating dinner!

Big yawns. . .

Love,
Lucie x

Dear Mum,

Today was my last guitar lesson with Mr Handford this term. He recorded three songs that I played and then made me listen back. I couldn't actually believe it was really me playing. I sounded pretty good. . .

Mr Handford was really pleased with my progress so far and said that I should practise as much as I can over the holidays. He said in September he can always tell the people who haven't lifted the guitar all summer. They waste weeks trying to catch up.

I love my guitar lessons, so will definitely make sure I practise over the summer, maybe with Dad. I'll try to take my guitar to France next month, if he lets me. Playing guitar makes me feel good and helps me to forget about things; all I need to concentrate on is the music.

The best part of the lesson was that Mr Handford said I was good enough to play in the school concert!

Dad's really pleased that I'm enjoying playing so much too. He got us two tickets for a guitar concert next week, just me and him. Chloe's annoyed, but I'm glad it's going to just be me and Dad for a change; besides, she doesn't even like that kind of music.

Love,
Lucie x

15th June

Mum,

It's my birthday and I just wish you were here, coming into the bedroom and singing 'Happy Birthday' to me like you used to.

It's so strange without you. I can't believe that today I am twelve and you're not here. . .

Dad said it's something to celebrate now that I am twelve. I suppose twelve is kind of grown-up.

Last year on my birthday you were so sick that we stayed home all day. Mémé came to stay for a few days with us and made me a special birthday dinner and a cake because you weren't well enough to cook . . . You were sad that you couldn't bake me a cake like you always used to, but at least we were all still together.

This year everything is different, but I'm glad that you are not sick and in pain any more. But I still miss you so much.

Before breakfast Dad gave me the special present you left for me.

It's so perfect . . . you knew that I'd love the pretty silver star and chain.

It made me think about us looking at the stars together. My little star is so beautiful. Dad said that even though you were very ill you bought it especially for me. I put it on straight away and promise that I will always wear it. Thank you!!

I got lots of other presents: Dad got me a proper case for my guitar, a new watch and some new trainers; Chloe got me a pink backpack with big daisies on it and a set of pink and white patterned writing paper and pens because I'm always writing; Hugo got me a DVD and made me an enormous card with butterflies and rainbows on it; Mémé and Pappa sent me a CD of wonderful guitar music and a t-shirt with *Le Musique* written on it and Granny got me a cookery book and has promised to take me into town to buy some new clothes. Even Mr Humphrey and Tess sent me a book token and a card.

I had my party after school and all the girls came over. It was really hot so Dad said he would barbecue.

We all sat out at the big table in the garden under the parasol. We were just talking and stuff when Dad and Hugo came out and squirted us with water pistols! Everyone was screaming and jumping around the place. Next thing Dad came back with a big bag of water pistols already filled with water.

Everyone grabbed one, and we had the best fun chasing each other and getting soaking wet. Eventually Dad said GAME UP and managed to get all the pistols back. Then we all sat out on the grass to dry off and Chloe made us yummy coke floats.

Everyone said it was a great party.

Amy stayed the night. She said our family are cool compared to hers. Her mum thinks it is easier to just go to the cinema for parties so that there is no mess to clean up at home.

I got out my guitar and tried to show Amy how to play some chords. Dad heard me play and came in with his guitar and we played 'Dancing in the Moonlight' together.

It was a really great birthday. The only thing that would have made it more perfect would have been if you were here to share it with me.

Love,

Lucie x

P.S. I really do love my silver star.

20th June

Mum,

Last night I had a strange dream.

I was lost in a big forest and I kept calling and calling
for someone to find me, but I was all alone. I wanted you.

I shouted and called, but you didn't come.

It was so dark and scary. There was a wolf in the forest
and I could hear him howling and searching for me. He
kept getting nearer and nearer and I kept trying to hide
from him, not even breathing in case he'd find me.

The wolf was so near I could feel his breath and then
I knew I had to run. I couldn't hide any longer. I ran so
fast and jumped so high I nearly went over the treetops. I
didn't look back and I kept running through the darkness
with the wolf still chasing me. . .

I woke up with a jump and then I was sure I heard you
say, *'It's all right, Lucie. The wolf is gone'*.

I tried to open my eyes to see you, but I couldn't.

All I could hear was your voice.

Gone . . . Gone . . . Gone!

It really upset me . . . but I knew you had come to make me feel safe.

Love,
Lucie x

21st June

Hi Mum,

The concert tonight was brill!

It was in a little theatre in town and just listening to guitars all night was so cool. The music was amazing and Roberto and Julia played everything from the Beatles to Roderigo's Concerto. Rock and classic. Dad and I loved it and it made me want to play and practice even more.

Mr Handford was there with his girlfriend so Dad finally got to meet him.

It was nice going somewhere on my own with Dad and listening to music that we both love.

Bonne nuit,

Love,

Lucie x

22nd June

Mum,

Natalie told us about her dad losing his job a few months ago. Now they have sold their house and are moving to Australia or Canada where her dad will find it easier to get a job. She's said that moving is the worst thing that has ever happened to her. All the other girls felt really bad for Natalie, but I didn't say anything. Even though it's sad that she'll be leaving us all behind at least her family will still be together.

Jess is upset too. Now that her parents are getting a divorce she's going on two separate holidays, one with her mum and one with her dad. She hoped if they went on a family holiday together her mum and dad might get back together, but now it doesn't seem like that is ever going to happen.

I know your mum and dad getting divorced must be terrible, but at least Jess still gets to see her dad every week and can talk to him on the phone. I can't ever talk to you on the phone or see you again!

Sometimes I don't know what to say to my friends. Because I really know what the worst thing in life is . . . it's losing your mum.

Why did the worst thing that can happen to anyone happen to us?

It's not fair. . .

You are gone and will never come back.

I miss you every single day.

Love,

Lucie x

29th June

Dear Mum,

We started our summer holidays today! Yippee!

I got a book token from Mr Humphrey's shop and gave it to Mrs Martin. She is the nicest teacher ever and I will miss her when I have a new teacher next year.

We had our Sports Day on Saturday and Dad and Chloe and Granny came along. Amy and I did the three-legged race and we were laughing so much we nearly fell and came second to last. Hugo won the egg-and-spoon race and his class running race! He's so fast!

Dad ran in the dads' race; he was brilliant and came fifth.

I kept thinking about last year and how even though you were really sick you still came and cheered us all on. I miss you so much.

Love,

Lucie x

Dear Mum,

I love summer!

It's really hot so Dad took us to Brittas Bay today. The beach was crowded, but we had a great time. We all had a swim, even Chloe, then she and Dad sunbathed while Hugo and I went off and explored the sand dunes.

We brought the red picnic box with us and had sandwiches and crisps and some drinks. Chloe's face and shoulders got really burnt.

We stayed on the beach till it got late and we all went for a last swim. The water was freezing, but it was brilliant.

We got fish and chips on the way home, but we were so hungry that we couldn't wait till we got home so we ate them in the car.

It was nice to spend time with all of us together, but
I know we were all wishing you were with us on the
beach today too.

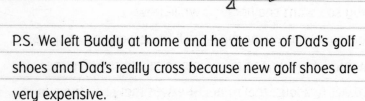

Love,
Lucie x

P.S. We left Buddy at home and he ate one of Dad's golf
shoes and Dad's really cross because new golf shoes are
very expensive.

4th July

Mum,

I went to see Anna today.

She is going on holiday next week and then we'll be away so I won't see her for a while now.

She said I have done really well these past few months, but that if I feel I need to come and talk to her after the summer holidays, that's fine. She said that she's there to help me feel less sad and lonely without you, and that I need to make sure I give myself enough time to 'deal with my feelings'.

I really like talking to Anna and it does help me cope without you. I think I will go back in September.

I will always love you, Mum.

Love,
Lucie x

Mum,

The weather is still scorching hot. Every night I water all the flowers in the pots and the flower bed as I don't want them to die.

The garden looks beautiful with roses and daisies and lavender and all your flowers everywhere. I know you would love it and I want to keep it nice for you.

Love,
Lucie x

7th July

Dear Mum,

   We all went to Eddie Rocket's this evening to say goodbye to Natalie, as she is going to Canada on Monday. Everything is packed up and her mum and dad have sold their house already.

   Natalie was trying not to cry; we all were as we might never get to see her again. She's really nervous and worried that she won't make any friends there.

   It feels like we've been friends forever so I'm going to really miss her. Amy has Skype on her computer and she says that I can come over every week and we can Skype Natalie, so we can keep in touch.

   We gave Natalie a big photo album with lots of photos of us all and a friendship ring. We were all crying so much that the waitress came over to ask if everything was OK.

   After dinner we walked back to Natalie's and sat in her kitchen chatting until we all got collected. Nearly all her furniture and stuff is packed up and the house looked really weird.

It was awful saying goodbye to her. . . Mum, if you can, will you try and help her make a friend when she gets there . . . please?

Love,
Lucie x

Tuesday 10th July

Mum – *vive les vacances!*

Today we flew to Paris and Poppa met us at the airport.
Dad didn't come with us – he's coming in a couple of
weeks as he has to work, but we were allowed to fly on
our own because Chloe is sixteen. She kept bossing us
around like she was so grown-up and in charge of us. I
read a book and Hugo played a game on his DS the whole
flight until we touched down.

Mémé got all upset when she saw us and I know it was
strange for her that we were on our own. It's strange for
us too. When we got back to the apartment she made us
our favourite chicken casserole and there was caramel
and chocolate ice cream for dessert.

It's good to be back in Paris, even if Chloe and I have to
share a bedroom. She's so annoying and has taken over
most of the space in the room and filled the wardrobe
with her clothes. Chloe and I are sleeping in your old
room . . . it makes me feel maybe you are here with us
when I see your things on the wall and on the shelves.

Tomorrow we are going shopping. Hugo's clothes all seem too small for him. His trousers, his jumpers and even his socks! Poor Hugo – no one had noticed.

'He's a growing boy,' laughed Poppa. 'You see him every day so maybe you don't see it so much, but your grandmother and I notice every change in you . . . in you all.'

I keep looking in the mirror to see if there is any change in me. But I think I still look the same: pale with freckles and white skin and hair that has a mind of its own. I wish that I was prettier like you or Chloe, but I guess I look a lot like Dad.

Mémé made us hot chocolate before we went to bed and kissed us goodnight. I love Mémé and wish that she lived nearer us then we could see her more often.

Bonne nuit.

Love,

Lucie x

P.S. Dad let me bring my guitar!

Mum,

Today we all went shopping.

We went to *Galeries Lafayette*, *Printemps* and all the big stores. Mémé made poor Hugo try on shorts and T-shirts and trousers and jeans and jumpers and even swimming shorts. She kept saying how expensive children's clothes are nowadays.

Chloe and I tried on a pair of cut-off jeans each and Mémé bought them for us too.

When were all too tired to shop anymore Mémé took us to the café near the Opera House and we had *crêpes* and chocolate ice cream . . . delish!

Poppa made dinner when we got home and we played cards till bedtime.

Paris is so different without you!

Love,
Lucie x

Dear Mum,

Chloe and I went shopping again today. My feet are sore from all the walking!

We went to the market up near Montmartre, Mémé said it was one of your favourite places. One stall had all print dresses and cute skirts and I got a short skirt with black kittens on it and Chloe's has little birds on it. I got sandals and blue shorts and a striped T-shirt and a red sweatshirt. We got a sundress each too.

Mémé said this was her treat for her beautiful granddaughters and that it made her happy doing things with us that you would have done.

Afterwards we sat in a café to rest and Mémé got the waiter to bring us cold drinks and a big *salade verte* and *frites*. Then we got the metro back to the apartment.

Hugo went over to stay at Uncle Theo's tonight so he could spend time with Mathieu and Max, so Mémé and Poppa took Chloe and I out for a special dinner. Mémé and Poppa met a few of their friends who all came over and said how sorry they were and how much they missed our maman. French people are good at saying how they feel about things, so Chloe and I thanked them. We stayed till very late and I was falling asleep in my chair when Poppa said we must go home.

I love Paris at night when it is all lit up and you can see inside people's apartments and the light from the Eiffel Tower seems to flash up into the sky and all around the city.

'Well, would you like to live in Paris then?' Chloe asked me, when we got back.

'Stay here? Live with Mémé and Poppa?' I do love Mémé and Poppa, but I love home too and Dad and our house and our road and my school and my friends. Paris is beautiful, it's probably the most beautiful city in the world, but it's not home. I wondered why Chloe would ask me that. . . Does she want to move here with Mémé and Poppa?

Love,
Lucie x

13th July

Dear Mum,

Poppa took us to the *Cité des Sciences* museum today as they have a big exhibition of robots and stuff from 'Star Wars' and 'The Terminator' and 'X-Men', as well as all kinds of games that we could test out. It was the best ever and Hugo got the highest score on one of the machines. He wants to be a games designer when he's older. Poppa liked the games too and said maybe he should buy himself a console!

Tonight we all went to Uncle Theo's apartment for dinner. Hugo stayed with Mathieu and Max again tonight. They have a huge bedroom and lots of really cool games and gadgets. Chloe says they are so spoilt even though they are our cousins.

Afterwards we went to a massive firework display as tomorrow is Bastille Day. It was amazing and all the streets and cafés were crowded with people watching the fireworks light up the sky. We sat outside till midnight.

Love,
Lucie x

Saturday 14th July

Dear Mum

It's Bastille Day. Everywhere was crowded! So we just lazed around and went to listen to the music and the bands playing in the park.

We all had dinner in Poppa's friend Olivier's restaurant which is near the river. There were more fireworks and a big party on one of the boats.

When we got back to the apartment I sat out on the balcony listening to the traffic below. Sitting alone in the dark I smelled your perfume, and I knew you were there too on the balcony with me, watching the lights come up all over the city you love so much.

You are home.

Love,
Lucie x

Chere Maman,

Today we drove all the way to Les Sables. Poppa and Mémé were arguing, as always, about where all the bags and boxes and my guitar should go. We left Paris after *le petit déjeuner* and only stopped a few times for lunch and coffee and to get petrol because we had such a long way to go.

It was almost dark when we arrived.

I have the small bedroom with the window overlooking the path to the garden. Someone had opened the window and there was a lizard in my room; he was only a baby lizard so he was quite cute!

It's great to be back at the old house in Les Sables and smell the sea and hear the waves. I can't believe that it is two years since we were here. Nothing has really changed except there is a new TV and Poppa has painted the chairs on the porch blue. Everything is still the same as you remember it.

Poppa says tomorrow we will go for a swim before

breakfast and that he is going to teach us all how to catch
a fish when we go out in his old boat.

I'm too tired to write any more.

I can hear the sea – the waves are rolling in and out, in
and out on the sand. *Bonne nuit.*

Love,

Lucie x

17th July

Mum,

I love this house. We all do and know you loved it too. When I am in this house I feel connected to you. Every summer you came here. You slept in the same bed I am sleeping in and listened to the same waves. Your clothes hung in the same wardrobe. There is an old yellow beach wrap hanging there and I wonder if it's yours. There are some old books of yours still on the bookshelf and some shells, and a painting of the beach that you did when you were twelve hanging over the bed and a snowglobe of Babar the elephant on the dressing table. The room smells of sea and sand and of you. . .

Poppa is happy to just go down to the beach in his shorts and sandals and sunhat, swimming or reading his papers and books. He's got his old boat tied up on the jetty so he can go fishing whenever he wants.

Mémé loves to relax in the garden and has a shady spot where she naps. Everything is just the same; nothing has changed except for you . . . not being here.

My freckles have all come out. I'm hoping the dots will all join up so it will look like I have a tan. Chloe puts lots of oil all over her self every day and has gone really brown. It's not fair that she gets such a great tan when I don't.

The next-door neighbours, the Vartans, came down yesterday. Madame Vartan gave me a big hug. She smelled of perfume and mints and told me that I'm a young lady now and am old enough to call her Marianne and not Madame Vartan any more.

Their two boys, Paul and Toma, are here too. They are all staying until the end of August. Monsieur Vartan has brought down his big boat and they promised to take us out sailing in it.

Toma has got really tall and even though he is the same age as me he looks older somehow. He tells lots of jokes and is really funny. He's asked me and Hugo to go with him tomorrow to look for crabs on the beach.

Love,
Lucie

Mum

Today we went out on the Vartans' big yacht. Marianne brought enough food for everyone to share. Their boat is huge and Toma says he often sleeps on it. It must be kind of cool to sleep on a boat and feel the sea and tide under you.

We sailed round the bay first and then Monsieur Vartan took us out in the open water. He let me take the wheel and it was brilliant trying to steer and turn the boat. We all had turns except for Mémé who said that she is a bad enough driver without going and crashing a boat! Toma steered the boat for ages.

Then we dropped anchor, went swimming and did some fishing. Poppa caught a really big fish - a sea bream which we ate for dinner tonight. I didn't catch anything, but I was glad as I always throw the fish back because I feel bad.

It was a bit scary swimming in the sea so far out as your feet could never touch the bottom. Hugo practised diving off the boat with Toma and Paul while Chloe and I just swam around. Then we all had lunch out on the deck.

Chloe kept trying to talk to Paul even though he is nearly two years older than her. She says he is very different from Irish boys and much better looking. I think he's kind of boring as all he did was listen to his iPod. Toma is much more fun.

I loved being out in the boat. Toma says his dad will bring us all out together again or else I can come with him and his dad when they go fishing.

Today was a really good day!

Love,
Lucie (your *petite* sailor!)

Tuesday 24th July

Dear Mum,

You won't believe it! Chloe is in love again. This time it's with Paul. Can you believe it?! She is mad about him and they keep hanging out together and telling Toma and me to get lost. How can we get lost on the beach or at the house! They are always hanging around together listening to music or watching DVDs or going for walks on their own. Mémé says it is just a holiday romance and that girls Chloe's age who go on holiday always need a little romance, and to have a handsome boy fall in love with them.

Chloe won't come to the beach or go fishing or shopping or anything unless she thinks that Paul is coming too. All she does is talk about Paul and listen to two or three yucky French love songs all the time. She's become kind of boring and pathetic! We are fed up of them. Hugo says it is gross.

Also, she won't eat anything as she says French girls are really skinny and she needs to be skinny too for Paul!

Mémé says Chloe is far too thin. I didn't tell her about Dr Wendy or what Dad said. Every day Chloe sits at the table and moves the food around her plate and either leaves it or puts it in the bin. Soon she will be even skinnier just because of stupid Paul. Mémé is worried that Chloe might be anorexic. She told us that French girls might be thin, but they are never scrawny because who wants to have bad hair, and skin and teeth, and look old!

Toma and I have started hanging out too and sometimes Hugo hangs out with us. I think all three of us want to escape from Chloe and Paul being so loved-up! There aren't many kids Hugo's age here yet, but Poppa says that the Silvanos' grandchildren will be coming at the weekend for a few weeks and he thinks that there is a girl about his age, and Uncle Theo and the boys should be here early next week.

Most of the time we go exploring and make maps and have big treasure hunts all around the beach and sand dunes hiding things and food. It's fun. Nearly every day we have a picnic or we go fishing with Poppa in his boat. I caught a big eel yesterday, but I let it go.

Today Toma let me try out his bodyboard when we went

to the beach. It is really hard to stay up on it as the waves just kept knocking me over. Toma can stay up on it for ages without falling off – he's really good at it. He said that tomorrow I can try it again and he'll show me how to stay on for longer. Toma is the nicest boy I know.

Love,
Lucie x

Dear Mum,

Today Hugo and I were helping Poppa to clean out his shed when we found a broken old canoe in the back. There is a big hole in it. Poppa said that it used to be yours and that you and Uncle Theo were great canoeists when you were younger. Poppa promised to try and repair it so that Hugo and I can use it.

Tonight we had dinner at the Vartans' house. We had some fish that Monsieur Vartan caught and there were strawberries and ice cream for dessert. Chloe was really polite to Marianne and even asked if she could help with the cooking. She ate everything on her plate too. I think Mémé noticed as well because she kept watching Chloe while she was eating. Afterwards the grown-ups showed us how to play bridge and gin rummy. Marianne said that she will teach Dad how to play when he comes here next week.

We stayed really late as Poppa and Mémé wanted to

play another hand of cards. Chloe made hot chocolate for Hugo, me, Paul and Toma and then she and Paul went and sat out on the porch on their own and told us all to stay inside!

Tomorrow Toma and Hugo and I are going out in their boat again. Hurray!

Bonne nuit.

Love,
Lucie x

Mum,

It's sweltering hot here, but I'm using sun block, don't worry. I don't want to get sun burnt. I'm still pretty pale compared to everyone else, but I do have lots more freckles everywhere!.

Chloe is still getting thinner – her shorts are falling off and she's had to tie them on with one of Hugo's belts! But even though she's too thin being in love makes her look really beautiful!

Uncle Theo and Auntie Clara arrived with the boys yesterday. They are all staying in the annexe. This morning Mémé, Aunt Clara and I went to the market and Mémé bought me a new pair of flip-flops and a T-shirt. It was crowded there and you know Mémé, she argued with all the stallholders to get a bargain: the peppers, the salad, the onions, the fish, the cheese, the tomatoes, the chillis, the pastries, the clothes . . . everything must be a bit cheaper! Afterwards we went to the café on the square for coffee and I had a pain au chocolat.

When we came home I went for a swim with the boys. Toma and Paul were there too, and Isabel, the Sylvanos' granddaughter. She's the same age as Hugo and lives in Rome.

We stayed on the beach until Uncle Theo called us to say dinner was ready. He cooked a big Mexican feast for everyone – it was delicious! There were meatballs and chicken and enchiladas, and I think Uncle Theo must have put a bit too much chilli in the meatballs as Poppa's eyes were watering and Chloe got a bad cough. It was so funny watching everyone grabbing glasses of cold water and gulping them down. Then we had a competition to eat another meatball and see who could last the longest without having to take a drink . . . Auntie Clara won – she said she's used to Uncle Theo's cooking!

We stayed up really late, sitting outside and talking. I even got my guitar out and we all sang together. Mémé said it was wonderful to have her family around her and that she felt you were here with us all.

Were you with us, Mum? Listening to the singing? Smelling the hot chilli?

I wish that you could give a sign. . .

I wish I was like that lady on TV that can see ghosts and talk to them, then I could talk to you all the time.

Love,
Lucie

Dear Mum,

Dad arrived today. He has the spare room, so now Hugo has to share my room. Chloe says she's not sharing with me . . . I don't want to share with her either, so it's okay having Hugo with me. Buddy has gone to stay with Granddad and Granny while we are in France.

Coming to the summer house made Dad sad and he went down to the beach for a very long time this afternoon. Mémé told Hugo and me to go down and remind him to come back up for dinner.

'Everything is the same,' he said hugging us, but then he looked back up at the house again. 'But at the same time everything has changed . . . without your mum, nothing can ever really be the same again.'

I know nothing will be the same again . . . no matter what we all do it never will be.

Poppa showed Dad the old canoe, and Dad promised to help him fix it. Hugo and I hope it won't take too long as we both want to try it out. I can't wait for Toma to see it.

Tonight we played cards and watched a silly film. I'm glad Dad's here. He needs a holiday. He looks tired and fell asleep watching TV.

Tomorrow we are having a big picnic on the beach.

Love,

Lucie x

Dear Mum,

We had a barbecue on the beach tonight.

Chloe looks so pretty. Her hair has got really long and she is so tanned.

She went to the big market in town yesterday with Paul and he bought her a silver bracelet with their two initials on it. C & P. It's so cool and I know she loves it because she keeps flashing it around.

The Vartans' came to the barbecue too and we stayed down on the beach till midnight. It was such fun, sitting on the sand, listening to the waves with everyone talking and laughing.

Love,
Lucie x

Mum,

Poppa and Dad worked on the canoe all day yesterday and now it's fixed

Hugo and I couldn't wait to try it out on the water so we all went down to the beach after breakfast to test it out.

Chloe wanted to have the first go, but Poppa said that wouldn't be fair as she has shown no interest in it up till now and is probably only trying to show off to Paul. She went off in a huff pretending to sunbathe.

Poppa said he'd test it first to make sure that it is safe and isn't letting in water.

'Better an old man like me gets a bit of a soaking in it than one of you!' he said. He took the canoe out really far and it was fine. Poppa's really good at canoeing and he told me he taught you and Uncle Theo.

Hugo went next. Dad and Poppa had to help him as he kept going round and round in circles. It was really funny. Poor Hugo!

When it was my turn I was really wobbly at first. It was

so embarrassing, I was worse than Hugo! Chloe kept laughing at me – she's so mean. I was going to get out and let Max have a turn when Poppa came over and showed me what to do. He told me that you were the same your first time in a canoe, but that you were soon better than Uncle Theo (although he told me not to tell Uncle Theo that he said that)!

Try . . . try again. You were always telling me that, so instead of giving up I tried again and I managed to get the canoe to go straight, then I paddled up by the boat slip, and then turned round and came back. Canoeing is brilliant. I love the feeling of the canoe moving through the water and the feel of the paddle as it hits it and how fast and light you feel . . . I think that I'm going to be good at it like you!

The boys were next. Then Chloe had a go. She paddled round in circles first too, but soon managed to keep it straight. She got bored really quickly and said canoeing is only for kids. Everyone had a turn – Uncle Theo, Dad and Auntie Clara.

Toma came along and was able to canoe first go. He said he went canoeing a few times before, up on one of the lakes with his cousin. He's so cool and loves being in the water. He's got the longest eyelashes and brownest eyes ever. . .

I stayed down on the beach for ages with Toma and the canoe.

I can't wait to try it again tomorrow.

Love,
Lucie (your little canoeist) x

Happy wedding anniversary!

Dad is sad today because it is your eighteenth wedding anniversary and you are not here to share it with him.

Poppa says that he should think of the happy years you had together and the three beautiful children you have.

Dad told us all about your wedding at the church in the village and the big party you had here at the beach house afterwards. He described all the candles and fairy lights you put up in the back garden and on the beach. Mémé got out the photo album to show us your wedding photos.

You were so pretty, with your long dark hair and long lacy dress and white flower in your hair. Chloe looks so like you. Dad looked a bit funny because he had been badly sunburnt, but you could see how much you were in love.

When I get married I'd love to get married here too.

Mémé put a photo of you and Dad up on the dresser.

Poppa said we need to remember Madeleine's good and

happy times not just the sad time when she left us.

You are so beautiful, Mum.

Love,
Lucie x

Mum,

I canoed right up along by the woods near the edge of the beach this morning. Then I went out near Petite Chèvre, the little beach you used to take us to. It was amazing . . . and once I got into the rhythm I got faster and faster. The canoe was flying through the water.

Dad stood on the beach watching me in case I got into trouble or the canoe overturned. He showed me how to do a rollover in the canoe and to get out of it. He told me that learning to fall out of the canoe safely is as important as learning to canoe in a straight line!

Sometimes when I am out on the water I wish that I could stay there forever and never go back to shore . . . that I was some kind of mermaid and not really human, like the mermaid in the story you used to read to us. But I wouldn't want to be a human. I'd stay a mermaid forever!

Hugo loves the canoe too and even Dad loves to go off on his own in it.

Uncle Theo bought an inflatable dinghy for the boys,

and then we all have Poppa's boat. This summer is the best ever with everyone spending most of their time in the water. Chloe doesn't like the canoe, but she and Paul go out in Poppa's boat sometimes when he's not using it as they just want to 'be on their own'.

We have only ten days before we go back home. I can't believe it. Chloe and I don't want the holidays to end or to go back home!

Love,
Lucie x

Saturday 18th August

Dear Mum.

Tonight there was a big dinner at the house. The Vartans came too and old Madame Ricard who lives in the pink house near the end of the road.

There were sardines, crab and all kinds of fish and chicken and stuffed peppers and lots of other food. Poppa put all the tables together on the back porch and Chloe and I put candles everywhere. It looked really pretty.

We ate outside and lizards kept hopping on the table to see what was going on, but Hugo and the boys chased them away.

We all sat around eating and laughing and talking for hours. No one was tired or wanted to go to bed, not even old Madame Ricard. She is eighty years old and has had two new knees since the last time we saw her.

Tonight is the last Saturday we will be here as we are flying home on Friday. I wish that we could stay even longer. Toma and Paul aren't going home for almost two weeks! I'm going to miss Toma. He's the nicest boy I know.

Near the end of the night Mémé got upset – she always gets upset when she talks about you.

'Not tonight,' said Poppa. 'Please! Not tonight, Celine.'

'Why not tonight? The family are all gathered and our good friends. It is time to remember my Madeleine.'

Chloe looked over at me. We kept talking with the boys down our end of the table. We didn't want a big family row.

Mémé started talking about how you should have gone to see other specialists . . . doctors in England or America, or even France, instead of just staying in a small country like Ireland. Dad got upset. He was holding his wine glass so tight that I thought it was going to break. He said that you had the best doctors and that you just wanted to be at home, that travelling too far would have made you worse, but Mémé said that you might not have left us if you'd seen some more doctors.

I wasn't sure what to say or think. Would it have made a difference?

Dad said that you did see two doctors in Paris on your last visit to Mémé and Poppa, but they couldn't do anything either and you didn't want to tell Mémé that they'd seen someone because you knew she would get upset.

Mémé's eyes were filled with tears – she didn't know . . . Dad couldn't look at her, but she stood up and gave him a big hug and said she was sorry.

No one spoke for a while . . . I think we were all thinking about you and how much we missed you being with us.

Everyone is always thinking of you, Mum . . . they were sad tonight because they think you are far away, gone from us, but *I* know you are so close.

Tonight I was sure I could smell your perfume again and hear you humming a little song as we sat under the stars. . .

Love,
Lucie x

22nd August

Mum,

This morning I got up really early and went down to the shore and took the canoe out. The beach was empty; the only person around was Poppa who was up on the porch reading his book and enjoying his café.

I canoed out along the beach and went as fast as I could. There was nobody swimming or messing about on boats, just me and the water. I paddled so fast the paddles were barely touching the water as I skimmed along it.

I looked back towards the beach and you were standing there watching me. You looked so beautiful. Your hair was blowing in the breeze and you smiled at me. You were laughing and happy! The sun was on your hair and your arms and T-shirt. You waved at me. I turned and paddled back towards you. I went as fast as I could towards the sand to get near to you. You kept smiling and laughing as I canoed along, but once I got nearer to you . . . you just disappeared.

I pulled up the canoe and walked all along the sand

looking for you, but there were no footprints, no marks.
Nothing.

Mum, why didn't you wait for me?

Why?

Love,

Lucie x

23rd August

Dear Mum,

I wish the holidays could last forever; all of us here at Les Sables together.

Chloe says she wants to stay here. . . She doesn't want to say goodbye to Paul and go back home. She wants to stay in France with Mémé and Poppa.

I'm going to really miss Toma and Max and Mathieu, but it will be good to see Amy and Jess and some of my other friends when I go back to school.

Today Hugo and Max and Mathieu and Toma and Isabel and I made a giant castle on the beach. Dad and Marianne took lots of photos of us with our castle. The tide will wash it away tonight, but we all had fun making it. Even some of the little kids helped. Chloe and Paul just ignored us all and went off somewhere together.

Monsieur Vartan took us for a last sail in his boat before we go home tomorrow.

We had a picnic on board and went for a swim in the ocean. I'll miss the Vartans and their boat, but Toma says

I'll see them all next year when we come back again.

Tonight Mémé and Poppa took the whole family out for dinner in the little restaurant down near the fishing pier.

I had calamari and chocolate ice cream.

Everyone was a bit sad that we were leaving, but Poppa made us all promise we would come back again next year and the year after. He told Dad that the summer house will always be our home too.

Chloe barely ate before she disappeared off to meet Paul. It was after midnight when she came home and she was really upset and crying. She started yelling at Dad and woke us all up. . .

'I am not going back,' she shouted. 'I want to stay here with Poppa and Mémé.'

No one said anything for a minute and then Dad went over and tried to talk to her. He said that even if she'd stayed here for a few more days, Mémé and Poppa would be going back to Paris soon and she couldn't stay with them then.

Chloe looked at Mémé and asked if she could live with them in Paris. Mémé looked upset. I'm not sure that she and Poppa wanted Chloe to come and live with them. A holiday is one thing, but for a year!

'You do realise that the Vartans live in Rheims?' asked Poppa. 'It is far from Paris.'

'It's not just because of Paul that I want to stay,' Chloe said slowly. 'I just want things to stay the same, to be here in France, in the country that Mum loved. Maybe Paul and I can see each other some weekends. . .'

Mémé gave Chloe a hug. 'None of us want the summer to end, everyone feels a little the same, but you have the courage to say it. When you are a little older then you will come to stay with us . . . go to college to study in Paris if you want! But for now you must go home. You are a family. Madeleine would not want to see her family split apart.'

Chloe nodded. 'I know.' she said, blowing her nose on Poppa's big blue hankie.

I hope that Chloe will be OK. Sometimes she drives me crazy, but she's my big sister and I don't know what I'd do without her.

The end of the holidays is always so sad, isn't it! Were you sad every time you said goodbye to Les sables?

Love,
Lucie x

Dear Mum,

Today was our last day.

Dad and Hugo and I got up early and went out in the canoe. The beach was quiet. I paddled right up to the end of the beach and back. Dad took photos of Hugo and me in the canoe.

The summer is ending and people are beginning to go back home like us.

Mathieu and Max are lucky they have another few days here. Max says that he will take good care of the canoe and make sure that it is properly stored for us all to use next year when we come back.

Toma came down to say goodbye. He says that I am the nicest girl he knows.

He gave me a bracelet made of shells. He says it will remind me of this summer. Then he gave me a kiss! Well, a sort of kiss . . . his lips touched mine and then we both laughed. I liked him kissing me.

My very first kiss, Mum, can you believe it?!

I will really miss Toma. I really will cos he's the nicest boy ever . . . ever.

I hope I'll see him next year when we come for the summer.

After lunch Uncle Theo drove us to the airport. Mémé was too sad to come, so she said goodbye at the house. She and Poppa are coming to visit us next month at home, so at least it won't be too long until we see them again.

The plane was crowded. Chloe was sad and even though she kept her dark sunglasses on and pretended to sleep on the flight I could tell she was crying most of the time. She must really miss Paul. Hugo and I played games on his Game Boy till we landed.

It's strange to be home. The house seems lonely and empty. It was so quiet when we opened the door. Usually you rush around and open the windows and make us unpack and go around checking things and saying: 'It's great to be home! There's no place like home.' But it doesn't feel like home without you. It feels strange. Maybe we had forgotten the feeling because we were away on

holiday but now that we are back we notice it even more.
The house misses you. We miss you.

 Can you make the house feel better, do you think?
Please try.

Love,
Lucie x
P.S. Mum, did you have your very first kiss when you were
at Les Sables?
P.P.S. I really like Toma.

Saturday 25th August

Dear Mum,

Buddy came back today. He was so excited to see us all he ran around the house barking. Then he went out and ran all around the garden and chased a big wood pigeon that was sitting in the lilac tree.

Granny took really good care of him while we were away and she even taught him how to 'shake hands'. He's a really clever dog . . . sometimes.

Granny said we were all looking better than she had seen us for such a long time and that the few weeks in France had obviously done us all good. Granddad's new hip is working well and he can play golf again and they are going to Donegal next week on their holidays.

Love,

Lucie x

P.S. Toma texted me. Yippee. He misses me!!

Dear Mum,

I went over to Amy's and stayed for tea. Amy's family went to Spain for a week and then they went to their caravan in Wexford for three weeks. She said that Spain was really cool as there was a big swimming pool at their apartments, but it rained for nearly one whole week when they were in Wexford. Amy's mum and dad nearly went mad. They were going to go home as there was nothing to do in their caravan except play cards and go for drives, but then luckily it got sunny again!

'A boy kissed you . . . I can't believe it!' said Amy when I told her about Toma on the last day, and showed her my shell bracelet and his text message.

'He's a French boy.' I tried to explain to her how French boys are totally different to Irish boys, that they're not so annoying.

Amy's got all her school books already and a new skirt and blouse and school shoes. Dad better take me shopping before we go back to school as I tried on my old school shoes and they really squash my toes. This year I hope that I can sit next to Amy in class again. We are going to really miss Mrs Martin (who is the nicest teacher in the school!) and hope that we get someone like her. Mrs O'Hanlon is having a baby and is not coming back this year. Miss O'Donnell sometimes takes fifth or sixth class or else it could be Mrs Edmond. Everyone says that she gives lots of homework and shouts at her class and is a bit of a grump.

After tea we went up to the park and hung out. Megan was there; she heard that we are definitely getting Mrs Edmond. Her mum knows the principal so that's how she found out.

Amy and I sat on the wall outside her house talking about it for ages, wondering what we will do if grumpy Mrs Edmond gives us loads of homework. It's OK for her because her mum can help, but I won't have anyone as Chloe is always too busy and Dad is always too tired! So I'll always be in trouble. . .

Love (and hugs),

Lucie x

P.S. Mum, if you can do anything about teachers, please try and make sure that I don't get Mrs Edmond this year. I know it's real busy in heaven with lots of big important things going on all around the world, but this is important for me and Amy. Please try.

Dear Mum.

You won't believe it . . . but Dad went shopping!

We had to get our uniforms and school shoes and our school books for this year. Everybody else got theirs weeks ago! So Dad had to take us.

The shopping centre was busy and there were lots of people queuing for uniforms.

Hugo has got so tall since France he needs everything new, plus loads of school shirts. Chloe had to get a new school skirt and shirts and jumpers as all her clothes are far too big on her. Dad says he's not getting her new PE stuff or a tracksuit, and that too big or not, she will just have to make do with them.

He's told me that he's hoping Chloe's old uniform will fit me when I go to St Mark's next year as uniforms are so expensive. That's miles away and usually things that fit Chloe never, ever fit me. It's not fair that I always have to get her cast-offs.

My school skirt is too short, so I needed a new one too

and I got four school shirts because nobody remembers to do the washing, so we are always short of school shirts in the morning.

Dad nearly went mad when he saw how much it all cost.

Then we went to the shoe shop.

Dad hates shoe shops!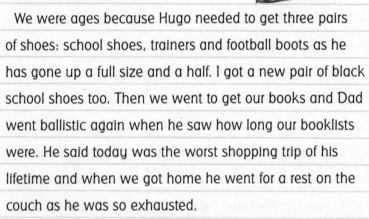

We were ages because Hugo needed to get three pairs of shoes: school shoes, trainers and football boots as he has gone up a full size and a half. I got a new pair of black school shoes too. Then we went to get our books and Dad went ballistic again when he saw how long our booklists were. He said today was the worst shopping trip of his lifetime and when we got home he went for a rest on the couch as he was so exhausted.

It's weird having Dad do the stuff you always did with us . . . and not half as much fun. I wish you were here.

Chloe and Hugo and I really miss you, Mum.

Love,

Lucie x

Mum,

I can't believe the summer is just about over and we're going back to school on Thursday.

Toma sent me a postcard of a yacht with its sails blowing as it races through the waves. He said he misses me. I miss him too. He is the nicest cutest boy I know.

Why does the summer always go so quickly? Too quickly!

Granny says that the summers seemed much longer when she was younger, and the days were always long and sunny and warm. But now the time is too short and everyone will be back in class at their desks and getting homework.

In heaven it is probably always summer. . .

Love,
Lucie x

Mum,

I can't sleep. I keep thinking about having Mrs Edmond.

I wish that you were here to talk to and that I didn't have to go back to school ever.

Chloe says it's after midnight and I'm just being crazy and that everyone gets bad teachers sometimes and you just have to get used to it and put up with it.

If you can do something . . . please do it.

Love (and yawns),

Lucie x

Mum,

You won't believe it, I've got Miss O'Donnell this year! She's *sooooo* nice! She got engaged in Italy during the summer and is getting married next summer. She showed us her engagement ring and said that we'd have to put up with a lot of wedding talk this year. Amy and I got desks beside each other near the window.

Mrs Martin, our teacher from last year, is teaching sixth class because Mr Gerard has retired and Mrs Edmond is teaching fourth class. Poor fourth class!

Hugo's lucky as he's got Mr Quinn and he's really nice too.

It's sad the holidays are over, but it's good to be back in school with my friends. Ben got braces, but he's still the cutest boy in class. Rebecca's mum is expecting a baby and Arianna and her family moved back to Poland, but we got a new girl from Nigeria in our class called Tia.

We all miss Natalie and hope she's happy in her new school in Toronto. Canada is so far away, but her dad's got a really good job there and Natalie likes her new house.

Carrie, the girl that lives next door to her, is in her class so she already has someone she knows at school.

Dad took us to Milano's after school to celebrate our first day back. Thanks, Mum (I bet you did have something to do with me getting Miss O'Donnell)!

Love,
Lucie xx

Autumn

Dear Mum,

Miss O'Donnell asked us to write an essay about something we hate.

She said it is easy to write about things we like, but a lot harder to write about things we don't.

It all started a big class argument about what we all hate the most.

The girls all hate rats, mice, spiders, snakes, earwigs and hairs in the plughole . . . gross.

The boys hate marmalade, medicine, perfume, nail varnish, vegetables, custard and hairspray and sisters! Stupid stuff mostly.

I didn't know what to write about first, but I know the thing I hate the most in the world. It's cancer. I even hate the word. I asked Chloe about it and she said she hates it too. So that's what I am going to write about.

I HATE CANCER.

Love,
Lucie x

Mum,

I don't know why, but I'm seeing you less and less . . .
sensing you less and less around me.

It feels like you are slipping away from me and I'm
worried that I won't get to see you any more.

When I think about you . . . I keep hoping I'll see you
at the bottom of my bed. Hear you, feel you . . . smell
your perfume but there is nothing, just the wall and the
wardrobe, the sound of my own breath and heart beating.

How long can a ghost stay?

Please don't leave. Not yet!

Love,

Lucie x

8th September

Dear Mum,

Amy and Jess came over after school yesterday and stayed the night. Lara made roast chicken and potatoes for dinner and said that we could make dessert.

Amy and Jess looked through your recipe book with me and thought it was really cool. Amy's mum keeps her recipes in a folder on her laptop, but Amy said a book was much better. We decided to make your yummiest chocolate desert, *Tarte à la Ganache*.

Dad and Hugo each had a big slice of the tart too and said how good it was.

After dinner we took Buddy for a walk up to the park.

I showed Amy and Jess the bracelet Toma gave me and his postcard and some of our holiday photos. They thought he looked really cute and that I'm cool cos I've got a French boyfriend!!

We played Fortunes before we went to sleep.

I am so lucky to have such good friends.

Love,
Lucie x

Chocolate Ganache

Ingredients
For the pastry:
175 grams plain flour
40 grams butter
40 grams margarine
2 tablespoons iced water
Pinch of salt

For the ganache filling:
300 grams sweet milk chocolate
312ml heavy cream
Smarties or M&Ms to decorate

Method
To make the pastry:
· Sift flour and salt into a mixing bowl. Cut the butter and margarine into small pieces and toss in the flour lightly. Rub them into the flour with your fingertips until the mixture looks like breadcrumbs.
· Add the water carefully to bind the mixture and use fingertips to shape into a firm but workable dough.
· Turn on to a floured surface and knead lightly till smooth and free from cracks.

- Lightly butter or grease a pie tin or flan dish, then roll out the pastry to fit the base and sides of the tin. Bake blind (put baking beans in centre of the pastry case to stop it rising while cooking) at 180 C. When cooked remove from the oven and let the pastry cool.

To make ganache:
- Break the chocolate into small pieces and place in a sturdy heat-resistant bowl.
- Pour the cream into a small saucepan and warm on medium heat. Remove from heat **as soon** as it comes to the boil.
- Pour the hot cream on top of the chocolate and cover the mixing bowl with a plate and let sit for 5 minutes.
- Using a wooden spoon stir the chocolate and cream until completely mixed.
- Pour into the cooled pastry shell.
- Refrigerate for at least an hour before serving. Decorate just before you serve with Smarties or M&M's.

Sunday 9th September

Mum,

Lara babysat for us last night as Chloe was going to the cinema with Sinead and Alex all her friends and Dad was going out. Lara went home last month to see her family; she said that it was so hot in Moldova that you could hardly go outside. I told her all about our canoe and how much fun we had in France, and how much I was missing Mémé and Poppa and everyone else. Lara said that she misses her family too, and that sometimes being away from people makes you realise even more how much you love them . . . I guess that's how I feel about you too.

I'm still going to book club this year and I think that Amy (though she's not really a great reader) and Jess might join too. Miss O'Donnell is big into books and hopes a lot more of the class will join. We are going to do a project called 'Write a Book' next term where everyone in the class will have to write and design and make a book. All the boys in the class just want to do a book about football or sport.

They are so pathetic and just copy each other.

Goodnight, sleep tight.

Love,

Lucie x

P.S. My guitar classes start again next week. I can't wait!

Happy Birthday Mum!

Last year you were too sick to enjoy your birthday.

It wasn't a good day. . . It was a really bad day.

Dr Nicholls called to see you and Liz, one of the nurses who came every day to care for you, was here too. She used to give you your injections to take away the pain and to help you sleep.

Sometimes you slept all day, but Dad put your bed facing towards the garden so that when you were awake you could see the trees and the flower beds and feel the sun.

Your poor arms were bruised from the injections and your bones sore from being in bed. You were so thin and pale and weak . . . it was as if bit by bit, day after day, we were losing you. Watching you get ready to leave us. . .

Mum, I'm glad that this year you're free of being sick and in pain, and I hope they have birthday cake in heaven! I really miss you, but have a Happy Birthday!

Love (and hugs and kisses),

Lucie xx

PS. I wish that I could see you.

Tuesday 11th September

Mum,

I auditioned to play my guitar in the school concert and you won't believe it . . . I got picked! I'm going to play one song and I have to decide which one. Jamie in my class has guitar lessons with Mr Handford too, and he got picked to play as well. Mr Handford said if our solo songs are good enough he might even let us play a duet! The concert is in November so I have to practise loads. It's going to be really hard to choose what to play!

Still can't believe it!

Auntie Trish's baby is due this week. Granny is saying lots of prayers for her.

Love,

Lucie x

12th September

Dear Mum,

Auntie Trish had a baby girl in the middle of the night. She's so cute and has dark hair and looks like a pixie. Uncle Alan sent us lots of photos of her. She weighs seven pounds and seven ounces and Auntie Trish is so happy. They are going to call her Sophie Madeleine, as Auntie Trish says that without you there would be no baby!

We are going to see her when Auntie Trish comes home from the hospital in a few days. I can't wait.

Dad says he'll take us to Dundrum town centre tonight and we can all pick something for the baby.

I want to get her a teddy and something pink. Isn't it lovely that we have a new little cousin!

I wish you could see her.
(But maybe you have!)

Love,
Lucie x

P.S. You and Sophie almost have the same birthday!

Thursday 13th September

Dear Mum,

   Mr Humphrey opened the new extension of the bookshop
tonight and we were invited to come along. There was
wine and orange juice and sparkling water and cheese on
sticks and crackers.

   The wine shop beside Village Books closed down over
the summer and Mr Humphrey took it over to join the two
shops into one bigger one with lots more space for books
and also for cards and gifts. Mr Humphrey says there will
be art exhibitions and book readings too, now that he has
a bit more room.

   It looks great. Roz and Johnny and Amy and her mum
and dad were there. My new teacher Miss O'Donnell was
there with her boyfriend Mike. She is so nice.

   I wish you could see the shop. The children's section is
much bigger and there are cushions and seats for kids to
sit down on and choose their books.

   Dad said we could buy a book each. We stayed on
ages after talking to Tess and Mr Humphrey. Tess said the
shop was really busy as nearly everybody bought books

tonight. Mr Humphrey said that everyone still really misses you in the shop and that he wishes you were here to see the changes he's made.

I got a new book called 'Secrets' which is about a brother and sister and a ghost.

Love,
Lucie xx

Friday 14th September

Dear Mum,

Yesterday we all gave in our essays about what we hate to Miss O'Donnell and today she read some of them in class. It's so weird some of the things people wrote about.

Amy did her essay on rats. I hate rats too as they are so disgusting and creepy and scary. Amy had a rat in her garden. It hid under her shed and her mum was too scared to even go out to the washing line or put stuff in their bins. Sean Kelly said he has a pet white rat called Finnegan and he's OK because he's a pet. But Amy and I said that we're never going to his house . . . ever.

Megan wrote about football and how she and her mum hate it because her dad and brothers are obsessed with it! They play football, watch football and talk about it all the time and her mum is always washing their dirty football gear.

Neil wrote about custard as his granny puts it on almost everything and Ben wrote about his mum's car which he says is an embarrassment. Do you remember she has that old pink mini that advertises her nail salon? I think it is cute.

Amir did an essay about cockroaches. When he lived in Turkey they had lots of them. It was so gross! I hope I don't have nightmares about them.

Tia wrote about prejudice. It must be hard coming to a new country and a new class and trying to make friends.

Simon did an essay about 'snot' which is the grossest thing ever, but Miss O'Donnell said it was rather funny. Three of the boys did ones on farting and belching . . . it's so typical of them.

Jess wrote about snakes. Her auntie got bitten by one when she was in Australia.

Miss O'Donnell didn't read out my essay, but she said it was one of the best and that it was written from very personal experience. She gave me an excellent! Amy only got a good for hers.

I thought you might like to read my essay too . . . here it is. . .

Love,
Lucie x

A+
excellent!

WHY I HATE CANCER

By

Lucie Ryan

My mum got cancer two years ago. She had a tiny lump and it got bigger and bigger. She had an operation and afterwards lots of medicines and treatment, but she still got sicker and sicker. The doctors tried special anti-cancer medicine on her, but that made her feel awful and all her hair and eyelashes and eyebrows fell out and she got sicker. Then the hospital and her doctor said that there was no treatment left. My mum got weaker and thinner and sleepier. Cancer had got her and wouldn't let her go. My mum died of cancer on 20th of September last year. I hate cancer.

People do not know that every day, every hour, someone's mum or dad or brother or sister gets cancer. Most people get better and are cured.

But sometimes, like a weed in the garden, cancer spreads and even though you try to pull it up, to kill it, to stop it, it keeps growing. Doctors and scientists are trying to find a cure for it. When I grow up I would like to be a scientist or a doctor and try to discover how to stop cancer and cure it.

15th September

Mum,

Sometimes I think about heaven and wonder what it is like up there.

Is it really all peaceful with white fluffy clouds and angels and people in long robes being good and kind to each other? Is it very crowded or is there space for everyone?

Do you have music and books and friends and fun in heaven?

Hugo thinks you are gone to a Galaxy far . . . far away. . .

Chloe says you are a speck in the universe and that's what we all become.

I'm not sure what I think, but I know you haven't gone too far away from us, that you are still close by . . . but even though I can feel you with me, it's not the same. . .

I wish that you were alive or you could just come back here to earth and to us.

It's a lot to wish for, but I do. . .

Love,
Lucie x

Mum,

We went to see baby Sophie Madeleine and she is the most beautiful baby ever! She's so tiny and when she grabbed my finger she wouldn't let it go. Her hair is black like Uncle Alan's, but I think she looks a lot like Auntie Trish.

We all took turns holding her and I helped Auntie Trish to change her wet nappy! Sophie is tiny and is sleeping in the Moses basket in the bedroom with Auntie Trish and Uncle Alan until she is old enough to stay in her own room. All her baby stuff is in the nursery; it's so sweet and has a wooden cot and is done up with balloons and clouds and her changing table and little wardrobe.

I got her the cutest little pink rabbit you ever saw with long ears; it's so soft and small that it will fit in her basket or cot. I got her a pink dress too. Chloe got her a zip-up fluffy suit and hat to wear in the buggy when she is going out for walks, and Hugo got her a pull-along wooden dog and a big packet of bibs. Dad is buying her a high chair for when she is a bit older.

Granny and Granddad came over while we were there and Granny says that having Sophie Madeleine is the best thing that has happened to this family in the past year. She said that new life coming into the world is precious.

While we were eating dinner Auntie Trish asked Chloe if she would like to be Sophie's godmother.

'If your mum was still with us I would have asked her, but Chloe, having you as our baby's godmother would be wonderful,' she said.

Chloe is so lucky! The christening won't be for ages, but I can't wait.

I hope someday I get to be a godmother too.

Love,
Lucie (and baby Sophie Madeleine) x

Dear Mum,

Today I went to Roz's after school and she asked if I
wanted to see the photos that she took of you last year.
I wasn't sure because I thought they might make me feel
too sad, but when I looked at them it was so lovely to see
you smiling and laughing, sitting holding your guitar, out
in the garden in your pyjamas, sitting on Dad's lap, you
and Hugo lying on the couch, Chloe putting on your nail
varnish, you brushing my hair. You asleep, you with no
scarf on your bald head, smiling, you dancing with Dad!

She spread them out so I could look at them and said
that she will give us some copies.

Roz said she cannot believe that it is almost a year since
you died, a year since she lost her best friend.

'Your mum and I talked a lot about how much she didn't
want to leave you, Lucie. Madeleine was frail and sick, but
all she talked and worried about was the three of you and
your dad. She couldn't bear it . . . having to leave you.'

Mum, I know you hated leaving us, but when I look at

the photos I can see that you were happy and I'm so glad that we were all together and that you are and will always be my beautiful mum.

Love and hugs,
Lucie x

Mum,

I saw you this morning. You were standing in the garden again, staring up at me. . . Your hair was blowing in the breeze and you were smiling at me. It looked like you were waving to me, as if you wanted to tell me something.

I opened the window, but then you were gone.

Love,

Lucie x

(Were you saying goodbye?)

19th September

Dear Mum,

Mémé and Poppa arrived this morning. They are here for your anniversary. Uncle Theo is coming later tonight.

Father Lennon is going to say a special mass for our family and our friends at church tomorrow.

Dad is upset. We all are. A year is such a short time and yet so long.

We cannot believe that it is twelve months since we saw you.

It's three hundred and sixty-five days since we said goodbye and you left us. I wish you could come back. . .

Love,
Lucie xx

My dear Lucie,

You are reading this letter a year after I have died.
   What a year for every one of us.
   This was such a hard letter to write knowing that I may never see you or speak to you, or touch or hold you again.
   You are my precious second daughter, my little music maker, bookworm and sunny soul with the kind heart. I know you will do your best to help Dad and Chloe and Hugo get through this terrible time. We are a family and even without me you still are. Lucie you are all surrounded by people who love you: Mémé, Poppa, Uncle Theo, Auntie Clara, Mathieu, Max, Granny, Granddad, Auntie Trish, Uncle Alan, Auntie Maria, Julie, Roz, Johnny and all our friends and family.

I wish that I could be with you to help you when you need me, in school, at home, as you grow up and study and go to college, and fall in love and marry and have babies of your own. I know I am missing out on so much, but I promise I will always be at your side, always there to help when you need me, to cheer when you do well and to soothe and support you when things go wrong. You will feel me when you need me and I promise never to desert you.

We don't live in a perfect world, unfortunately you have already discovered that, but life can be really good, so much better than we expect. . . Love is there for us if we only look, and happiness is waiting for us if we just grab it. Even though I've been so ill I have stayed so long just to be near you all for a little longer. It is so hard to leave you . . . to say goodbye . . . because I love you so much, but I'm sure there is another life. I have seen glimpses of it and I know that in time we will all be together again.

Know that you are loved. Know that I only left you because I had to. It is the hardest thing to say goodbye.

Be happy, be kind, be the wonderful daughter you always have been that I love so much.

Lucie, I promise I am never far away if you need me.

Words on the page can only say so much . . . you of all people know that.

Love always and forever,
Mum xx

20th September

Dear Mum,

This morning I read your letter.

I read it over and over again, before we went to the church.

I knew that you would leave a sign. . .

A letter, not just for me, but one for Dad and Chloe and Hugo too!

You always loved writing letters, putting your thoughts and words on the page, and you asked Roz to give us your letters today. We will keep them forever and read your words over and over again.

I know you are not far away and that you are always near if I need you.

You knew we would all need you so much today, Mum . . . going to your anniversary mass, standing at your grave and remembering, but you left us all a small part of you in your letters and I felt you were there with us.

When we all sat around the table eating together I know you were there, and when we were talking, laughing and crying about you I know you were there too.

When it began to get dark we went outside to the garden and Uncle Theo and Dad lit the big Chinese lantern and we all stood with our arms round each other watching it take off and lift and fly high, higher into the sky, burning brightly and flying away, away, away, till it became a small speck in the sky, I know you were there . . . saying goodbye.

I'm sad today, lonely without you. We all are, but I will try to be happy, try to be brave and strong and true and kind like you. I promise.

I will love you always, forever and ever and ever.

Love,
Lucie x

Acknowledgements

Thank you to my wonderful editor Jane Griffiths
for all her enthusiasm, energy and work on this book.
Thanks also to Venetia Gosling, Phil Earle,
Stephanie Purcell, Elisa Offord, Kathryn McKenna,
Jane Tait, Becky Peacock for their work on my book
and thanks to everyone at Simon & Schuster
for the warm welcome.

Thanks to artist Linzie Hunter, designer Paul Coomey,
Laura Hope (for the doodles) and Clara Chambers for her
lovely Mother's Day card illustration.

Thank you Simon Hess, Gill Hess,
Helen Gleed O'Connor and Declan Heaney and
all the team at Gill Hess, Dublin.

Thanks to my agent Caroline Sheldon for
her belief and constant encouragement.

A big 'Thank You' to the following schools
and teachers for their input into this book:
Sean Kelly and the pupils in
Kilrickle National School, Kilrickle,Co Galway.
Greystones Educate Together, Greystones, Co Wicklow.
Taney National School, Dundrum, Dublin 14.
Jean Coleman, and the girls in
St Brigids' Primary School, The Coombe, Dublin 2.
Norah Radford and the pupils of
Swords Educate Together, Swords, County Dublin.
Bean Ui Fhéich and Sixth and Fifth Classes
Scoil Lorcan, Monkstown, Co. Dublin.
Dolores Farrell, Laura Wickham and Laura Shields and
their classes in St Brigid's G.N.S Killester, Co Dublin.

Thanks also to the wonderful Sloweys: Sharon
and daughters Jane, Alison, Susan and Jill.

Thanks to writer Sarah Webb, for her unstinting support
and good advice, and for just being one of the nicest people
I know. Also thanks to her daughter Amy Rose.

Thanks to Kim Harte, for her generosity
in sharing her opinions with me.

Thanks to Ariane Menut for her green fingers,
her French recipe book and her wisdom.

Thanks to my family - my husband James and Mandy,
Laura, Fiona, James, Michael, Holly and Sam Hearty
and Michael Fahy. Special thanks also to my daughter
Fiona for her help with cover ideas.

Finally a huge 'Thank You' to all my readers - you are the best!

About the Author

Marita Conlon-McKenna is one of Ireland's bestselling novelists, writing both for children and adults. *Under The Hawthorne Tree*, her most successful children's book, has sold more than 500,000 copies and been translated into numerous languages. She has won several awards for her writing, including the prestigious International Reading Association Award, USA, and Ireland's Bisto Book of the Year award. Marita lives in Dublin with her husband.